JONAS

BEAUTIFUL DEAD

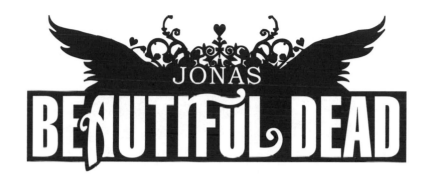

JONAS

BEAUTIFUL DEAD

Eden Maguire

sourcebooks
fire

Published by Sourcebooks Fire, an imprint of Sourcebooks, Inc.
P.O. Box 4410, Naperville, Illinois 60567–4410
(630) 961–3900
Fax: (630) 961–2168
www.sourcebooks.com

First published in Great Britain in 2009 by Hodder Children's Books.

Library of Congress Cataloging-in-Publication data is on file with the publisher.

Printed and bound in the United States of America.
VP 10 9 8 7 6 5 4 3 2

For my two beautiful daughters

1

The first thing I heard was a door banging in the wind. It spooked me because I didn't even know there was a house here among the trees, this far out of town.

Slow down, heart, I thought. *Darina girl, get a grip!* But back then a falling leaf would have spooked me. It was two days after Phoenix had died.

So the door banged and my heart thumped, and I was looking for something on that hill, I don't know what. I walked to the top and looked over the ridge and there it was—an old log-built, falling-down house with a porch, a big old barn, and one of those round water tanks on stilts, all rusty and decrepit. So was the truck parked at the front of the deserted house, with its fenders falling off and the roof caved in, and yellow grass growing knee-high around the porch.

It was the door of the barn that banged shut. Open-shut, open-shut, whenever the wind grabbed hold.

I guess most people would have walked away.

Not me. As I said before, I was lost and looking for answers to big questions about love, loss, and the meaning of life.

Darina on a mission, you might say. Like, how come four of my classmates at Ellerton High had died in the space of a year? Jonas, Arizona, Summer, and now Phoenix. I mean, how weird and tragic was that? It scared the hell out of everyone, I can tell you.

But the last one—Phoenix—broke my heart. I was in love with the guy, mostly from a distance. Then for two blissful months we were dating. My flower tribute to him, placed on the spot where he got stabbed, was pathetic. It read, "I'll miss you forever, with all my love, Darina" and didn't even scratch the surface of the way I felt.

So I was going to stop that barn door banging then take a look around the ghost house. I wanted to get inside, see how the people had lived—what plates they had put on their table, what chairs they had sat on.

But first the barn. The door was huge and held together by a hundred rusty nails. The inside was dark. I could see old horse halters hanging from hooks, a pair of dusty leather chaps, some cobwebby rakes, and brushes.

And a whole bunch of people standing in a circle, chanting a rhyme at a guy standing in the center. I didn't believe my eyes when I first saw him, but that guy was Phoenix, stripped to the waist as true as I stood there. Phoenix who had died from a knife wound between his shoulder blades. The knife had plunged through a major artery and he'd bled to death.

An older guy, with gray hair, stepped into the center of the circle and placed his arms on my dead boyfriend's shoulders.

"Welcome to our world," he said.

Bang! The door behind me slammed shut. I thought my heart was going to shudder to a halt.

"The world of the Beautiful Dead," the group chanted.

"You are one of us—welcome."

Phoenix—it was definitely him—looked out of it. Kind of dazed, as if he couldn't get his eyes to focus.

The gray-haired guy's hands steadied him. "You're back," he murmured.

"From beyond the grave," the group whispered.

I shook my head to make this stuff go away. *It can't be happening! It's some kind of stupid trick!*

Dead is dead, and you can't come back.

Except that the headshake made no difference and I was a witness.

"Hey, Phoenix, it's cool," a girl said, stepping up to him.

"Remember me?"

She had her back to me, so all I saw was her long dark hair.

"Dude, remember me?" A guy detached himself from the group, and then another girl, this one with fair hair falling over her shoulders.

"It's OK, Hunter fixed it for you," the blond girl explained. "This is Hunter."

The older, gray-haired guy offered to shake Phoenix's hand. "Not too much pain on the journey back?" he asked like a doctor checking on his patient.

"Nothing I couldn't handle," Phoenix replied.

It was *his* voice. Never more than a mumble—deep, kind of lazy. He eased his broad shoulders as if they hurt a little.

"Hunter looks out for us all."

The blond girl's smile pulled me in further. Hey, I knew that amazing warm smile, though the hair was longer, wilder, the skin paler. It was Summer Madison. I was watching another dead person walk, talk, smile.

"He brought us *all* back." The dark-haired girl joined in with the explanations. "Hunter's the boss man."

I was hearing but I wasn't looking at her or Hunter. My eyes were fixed on Phoenix. Truly, my heart couldn't keep on thumping like this without jumping clean out of my rib cage.

I wanted to run to him, touch him, kiss him, hold him in my arms. But I was totally freaked out.

"Why?" Phoenix wanted to know. He'd got his balance and his focus now and was suspicious. His gray-blue eyes narrowed to a frown.

"That's up to you." The "remember me" guy shrugged, and

I stopped staring at Phoenix long enough to catch a glimpse of his blue eyes and curvy, full mouth—Jonas Jonson.

"You're back here for your own reasons," Summer explained. "We all are."

"Where is this? What's happening?" Phoenix asked. Nothing made sense to him, or to me, spying from the outside.

"Get up to speed," the dark-haired girl laughed, but not unkindly. "Didn't you hear? You're one of us, the Beautiful Dead."

"Arizona?" Phoenix did the headshake thing, just like me. She was there, right in his face. "How come?"

"I have things to do," she replied with a toss of her head. "Stuff to put right."

Phoenix Rohr, Arizona Taylor, Summer Madison, and Jonas Jonson. The four dead kids from Ellerton High.

So beautiful, all of them, with their pale skin and their wild look. Not damaged by death.

Love and loss battered at my heart.

Bang! The door swung open and slammed shut.

Hunter was walking toward me. "I'll get it," he told the group. "We need to fix this latch. It's driving me crazy."

What can I say? I panicked.

I jumped out from the stall where I'd been hiding and made it to the door before Hunter. I didn't care if he saw me. I was out in the open and running past the deserted house, past the water tower, along the rough track between the aspen trees. I didn't even look over my shoulder.

"Where did you go?" Laura, my mom, was in my face the minute I slammed my car door.

I was walking up the driveway when she pounced.

"Nowhere. I drove someplace." I knew the answer would annoy her, but it was all I could come up with right then. It was better than, "I saw four dead people walking and talking."

"You can't just drive around," she nagged as I went up the steps and through the door. "You know the price of gas."

Silence from me. I threw my keys on the kitchen table. "Darina, I was worried about you."

"No need," I said, heading for my room.

Laura cut me off. "I *am* worried," she insisted. "You don't talk. You don't eat."

"I'm not hungry."

"Are you getting any sleep?"

Yeah, I'm sleeping right now and having a nightmare. Wake me up, someone!

"Darina, talk to me," she said.

I've never talked much to Mom, not since Jim moved in four years ago. There's nothing wrong with Jim, but not much right either. Mr. Bland Techie Guy, traveling around the state selling laptops.

"I know you're upset," Laura sighed.

Upset? Try "devastated," "wrecked," "ripped apart." Like someone made a hole in my heart, my head, whatever it is that makes me who I am. I stared at her and tried to stop my lip from trembling.

"It's his funeral on Tuesday," she said quietly. "Brandon came into the store yesterday to buy a dark jacket."

"Say his name, why can't you?" The pain made me angry. "His name is Phoenix!" *Was* Phoenix. *Is* Phoenix. Had I seen him at the barn or not?

Usually Laura would call me out on disrespectful stuff like this and it would end up in a fight. But today she let it go. "You want me to write to the principal and ask for the day out of school?"

I shrugged. I'd take it anyway. "I need to crash," I told her. My head was spinning. "If I don't get some sleep I'll go crazy." *Am* crazy already.

So Laura let me pass and I finally made it to my room. I flopped onto the bed and stared at the ceiling. I tried hard to block what I'd seen in the barn. I didn't really drive to Foxton and park the car, walk through the silver aspens with their golden leaves fluttering. Hear a door bang and walk over the ridge.

Rewind that part of the day. Go back to the afternoon I spent with Logan at his place, just sitting being silent and sad together.

"Phoenix wasn't the violent type," I said after an age of saying nothing. "He didn't get into fights."

Logan and I were out on his porch. There were empty Bud bottles lined up on the rail, his dad's dusty boots kicked off and lying under the swing. "Maybe you're right."

"We'd arranged to meet up," I went on. It was Friday. I'd been waiting for Phoenix in my car out by Deer Creek, watching for his truck as the sun went down, but he never showed. "So how come?" I asked Logan, letting tears slide down my cold cheeks. "What happened exactly?"

"They were all carrying knives," he told me gently. "Phoenix too."

I shook my head. "I don't want to hear that."

"It's true, Darina. Phoenix was no angel, believe me."

That's when I decided to leave. I got up and accidentally knocked over a couple of empty bottles. They smashed on a rock beneath the porch.

Logan followed me down the gravel path to the road. "How long were you and Phoenix an item?" he asked. "Six weeks, two months maybe?"

I wouldn't answer. My tears were angry now.

"So how well did you know him—*really* know him?"

I got in my car and slammed the door.

Logan leaned in and grabbed the steering wheel. "How long have you known me? All our lives. Trust me, Darina, I wouldn't tell you anything that wasn't God's honest truth."

"So what are you saying?" I shot back at him over the rev of the engine. "My boyfriend was a member of a gang who carried a knife and deserved to die?"

"No!" Logan shook his head furiously. "No more than Jonas deserved to crash his bike. Or Arizona to drown in the lake, or Summer…"

"Don't!" I yelled at him. Four deaths in one year. "No need to remind me, thanks. Now let go of the wheel."

We'd known each other since kindergarten, Logan Lavelle and I, but he was misreading this situation big time.

"I thought you'd understand," I flung at him as I stepped on the gas and shot away from his house.

Last Friday I'd waited an hour for Phoenix out at the creek. Then Logan had driven to find me. "There's a fight in town," he'd warned. "A big one. Brandon's involved. So is Phoenix."

I didn't believe what Logan was telling me until I'd broken all the speed limits on the road to Ellerton. I was mad at

Phoenix for not texting to tell me he couldn't make it. I was choked with worry that Phoenix's big brother, Brandon, might do something really crazy this time. Then I got to town, and it was too late. The fight was over. There was blood on the ground.

"I could get you some therapy," Laura offered as I left for school the next day. "I'll find the money somehow."

"Do I *look* as if I need therapy?" I snapped back.

She took a sharp intake of breath as I scooted out of the house, down the steps, and into my car. I made a list as I drove into town.

Major reasons to be unhappy: My parents split when I was twelve. My stepdad's a loser. My boring school sucks and there's a jinx on it that keeps getting people killed. My boyfriend just died…

Tears streamed down my face. I was broken and I couldn't see anyone around who could fix me.

Logan thought he could. He came up to me as I parked my car in the school parking lot. Tall, tanned, with dark brown curly hair—the hair that was golden when he was in preschool.

"Hey, Darina."

I slammed the car door. "Didn't we just have a fight?" I reminded him.

"Yeah, sorry about that. But you got it all wrong. I wasn't trying to say that Phoenix got what was coming."

We walked into school together, me slightly ahead of Logan, trying to tune him out. But his last remark got through to me. "That's what everyone else in Ellerton is saying though," I reminded him. "'Phoenix was just like Brandon. They were brothers, the same DNA, the same faulty genetic code.'"

"No, they're not. Don't get paranoid," Logan begged. He ran ahead of me and blocked my way down the corridor. "No, that came out wrong too. It wasn't a criticism. I mean, your feelings are totally mixed up right now. That's understandable. It's tough for you, I know it is."

I sighed and it came out like a groan. "Logan, I'm just trying to put one foot in front of the other. Please can we *not* talk?"

He nodded then gave way. "Text me if you need me," he called.

I walked into my classroom and for a split second I saw Phoenix sitting on the window ledge, his long legs stretched out across the table, his feet crossed at the ankles. He smiled at me.

I am crazy! I told myself for the hundredth time since Foxton.

Then I was surrounded. I lost sight of my ghost in the corner and there was a heap of touching and hugging. My boyfriend had just been stabbed to death. I was the flavor of the month.

That was before the special gathering in the school's state-of-the-art media center. The principal called all students together in the theater.

"We're meeting to share our sorrow at the sudden death this weekend of one of our senior students, Phoenix Rohr," Dr. Valenti began.

There wasn't a single person in Ellerton who hadn't already heard the news. I was sitting between Jordan and Hannah, staring straight ahead. They glanced sideways at me as if I was made of glass and someone might drop me.

"There's still a lot of confusion surrounding the circumstances of Phoenix's passing," Dr. Valenti went on, standing on the stage in his gray suit, using gray words. "But what we do know for sure is that he will be sadly missed by everyone here."

I heard a few people sobbing. I blinked and saw Phoenix standing right behind Dr. Valenti, smiling at me again.

Once, OK, it was just me being crazy. Twice, and I had to pay attention. My heart tried to storm its way through my rib cage.

The principal did his bland stuff. He told us we were going to have a minute's silence. "We'll bow our heads in respect," he said. "And while we think of Phoenix, we'll bring to mind the others we have lost this year. We'll remember Jonas, Arizona, and Summer, and I for one will keep them in my thoughts as I carry out the tasks ahead during this coming day."

One lousy day. How about a lifetime, Dr. Valenti?

I blinked again and Phoenix was gone.

Come back! I thought. But my heart soon stopped trying to force its way out. I knew I'd been seeing crazy stuff.

We all kept our heads down for exactly sixty seconds— then it was over.

"Stand up, Darina!" Jordan whispered in my ear.

Clunk went a thousand hinged seats as everyone stood up and filed out.

If you asked me about the rest of that day, I wouldn't remember a single thing. Friends spoke to me and I didn't hear. My math teacher suspected I was going to black out. She sent me to the school clinic. I lay on a bed and stared at the ceiling, hoping to see Phoenix's face in the shadows cast by the redwood tree outside the window. Hannah came to see me. I didn't speak. Nothing broke through.

All I knew was, if Phoenix wasn't going to show up again, I'd have to go and find him. I would drive back out to that old house and barn.

School finished and there was an obstacle in my way in the shape of Brandon Rohr. He was leaning against the side of my car, arms folded across his chest, waiting for me.

I tell you now, Brandon was Phoenix's brother but they were total opposites. They didn't even look alike, except they were both well over six feet tall. Brandon was the bulky football type, Phoenix was more the graceful basketball player. Brandon's hair was cropped close to his head, while Phoenix wore his hair longer, almost to his collar.

Brandon never smiled. Especially not now, three days after his brother died.

"Get in the car," he told me.

I fumbled with the lock and the ignition. Brandon sat down in the passenger seat. "Where are we going?" I asked.

"Just drive."

I took a deep breath then did as I was told. Soon we were heading west, out of town. I stopped my hands from shaking by holding tight to the steering wheel.

Brandon sat deep in the seat and laid his head against the rest. He closed his eyes. "So?" he mumbled.

"So?" I took a turn off the paved road and rattled off down a dirt track, toward Hartmann Lake, where Arizona had drowned.

"So, now's your chance to ask me some questions," Brandon replied. "Anything you like."

I frowned, not believing that compassion was Brandon's style. But I did want to know—so many blurred details.

"Phoenix—did he die right away?" My voice hardly qualified as a whisper. I had to ask the question three times before Brandon picked it up.

My memory burned with an image of the spot where I saw the blood on the road, outside the gas station.

"No, we got him to the hospital, but they couldn't bring him back."

"Was he conscious?"

Brandon shook his head. "Only for the first couple of minutes. He was losing blood fast, so he blacked out."

"Did he—did he say anything?"

"About you?" It made me sound mean and selfish, the way Brandon said it. And he didn't open his eyes.

"Yes. Did he mention me?"

Brandon stayed in the same position as we bumped and rattled toward the lake. "He asked me to come and talk to you."

"To say what?"

"Good-bye, I guess."

Good-bye. Two syllables. "Just that?" The lake spread out in front of us now, glimmering silver for miles either way.

"'Tell Darina I'm sorry.'" Brandon gave me the exact quote. He pulled himself upright and stared out at the water. "He made me promise."

My struggling heart rose up into my mouth. I couldn't speak anymore.

"Turn the car around," Brandon ordered after a whole silent minute of lake gazing. "Drive back to town."

"Who killed him?" I asked faintly as Brandon gestured for me to pull up outside his apartment block.

It was as if metal jaws had snapped shut and trapped all the information inside his head. Brandon shrugged. "I have no idea."

"But you were there. You saw it."

He shook his head. "Were you ever in a fight?"

"No."

"There were twelve or more guys. Kicking, punching, shoving. Someone pulled a knife. That's all I know."

Brandon stepped out of the car. He leaned one arm along the roof and lowered his head to look me in the eye. "We're holding a wake out at Deer Creek. Me and a bunch of my brother's buddies. It was Phoenix's favorite place."

"After the funeral?" I whispered.

He nodded and walked off.

I gripped the steering wheel and let my head fall forward. I sobbed.

A woman pushing a stroller walked by. She stopped, turned, and came back to speak to me. "How are you doing?"

I raised my head. "Good, thanks." Though it was plain obvious I wasn't.

"You sure? Do you need anything?"

I wiped my cheeks with the back of my hand. "No. I'm good."

The stranger hovered awhile longer. "Whatever it is, honey, it'll look better tomorrow. And the day after will look better still."

"Thanks," I told her. She was maybe seven or eight years older than me, with a baby and a life ahead of her—husband, more kids, a home. She smiled kindly, nodded, then walked on.

I was left with myself and my own crazy thoughts, rerunning events, longing to glance sideways and see Phoenix sitting in the passenger seat, smiling and saying, "Hey, Darina, drive this crappy car out of here, why don't you?"

"Where to?" I'd grin.

"Any place she'll make it to. Let's get the hell out of here!" he'd tell me.

And he'd slide his arm along my chewed-up driver's seat, put his feet on the dashboard, and lay right back.

I'd see his face in profile as I drove. His eyes would be closed, the wind would push his hair back from his face. I would be totally in love with him.

As it was, now that Brandon had gone, I was free to drive out to Foxton again.

Do it! I told myself. *What's holding you back?*

In my mind's eye I saw the empty house and the broken-down barn, heard the door banging and the rustle of the aspen leaves in the breeze. Maybe that's where it was and nowhere else—inside my unreliable, traumatized head. Did the house exist? How come I'd never come across it before, or ever heard anyone mention it?

Foxton wasn't that far out from Ellerton; maybe fifteen miles up a narrow road into the mountains. There were half a dozen houses at a small crossroads and a pokey local store that nobody ever used. Oh, and there were a few weekend shacks overlooking the creek, used by fishermen and hunters—city slickers mostly.

OK, so I could drive to Foxton and check things out. I could ask in the store if they knew about the house in the aspens. It seemed like a plan, so I set off.

Not much of a plan, as it turned out. I pulled up at the Foxton store and found it closed for business and a hand-written For Sale notice taped inside the window. Grit blew across the dirt road and into my eyes so I got back into the car. I was expecting tumbleweeds and lonely guitar music, like in Clint Eastwood movies.

"Shoot!" I turned the key and heard the engine splutter. The gas gauge showed empty. I hadn't even been paying attention… "Always carry spare gas in the trunk," boring Jim would say. "You never know when you might run out."

Jim would have been right.

I rejected the obvious choice of calling Laura on my cell phone. She'd be mad as hell with me, and it would mean the end of my expedition out to the old house.

I got out of the car again and thought hard about other options. Hitch a ride to the nearest gas station? Yeah, and get picked up by some psycho—too risky. Call a buddy and plead for help? It seemed too pathetic. Plus, they'd start asking questions.

"Hey, Darina," someone called out.

I recognized Mr. Madison as he pulled off the road in his silver SUV. He was Summer's dad, still taking time off his work as an architect to help his wife handle the grief of their daughter's death. He looked pale and drawn as he stepped down from his vehicle. "You got a problem?" he asked.

"Clean out of gas," I admitted.

He nodded. "I lost count of the times I told Summer to check she had a gas can in the trunk."

"I know. I'm so dumb."

"She never listened either. Kids, huh?"

I felt guilty for still breathing, poor guy.

"Lucky I came along," Mr. Madison said, fetching a green can from the back of his car. He unscrewed the nozzle and the strong smell of gas hit my nostrils. I watched him pour the clear liquid into my tank. "This'll get you home."

"Thanks." I breathed, avoiding meeting his gaze, remembering all the blue-sky evenings I'd spent at the Madisons' untidy, arty, friendly, out-of-town house before Summer… well, when Summer was alive.

"You're welcome," he said with a faint smile. "Turn the ignition—make sure you're OK."

I did as Mr. Madison said. The engine started up. I was good to go.

"OK," he said, climbing back into his car. "Glad I came by. Take care, Darina." And he drove off.

I could've said, "I'm on my way to see Summer's ghost, Mr. Madison. She's up there, along the dirt road, in a derelict barn. Along with Jonas, Arizona, and Phoenix. All of them together, calling themselves the Beautiful Dead. The fact that you're here right now is kind of fate. Why not come along?"

But his heart was already broken and I suspected that what I had to offer was pure, grief-fueled craziness. So I watched his SUV disappear down the road.

And now I had no obstacles left—I had to drive on, up

the dirt track past the weekend hunters' and fishermen's shacks perched on jagged granite rocks overlooking the fast running creek, on into the pine forest with the heavy, scented boughs. Then I was out of the long shadows onto a clear road zigzagging up the mountain to the aspens ahead.

My car bumped over boulders. The tires crunched over gravel and skidded around tight bends. There were no houses, no other vehicles, just a big evening sky and a pale moon rising.

Still no house, I thought when it felt like I'd driven far enough. *And no barn.* I searched for the place where I had parked my car the day before. A couple of hundred yards farther along, I decided, slowing a little and trying to recognize landmarks.

Then I came to a bunch of trees and saw a narrow track to my left. In the long grass, a mule deer raised its startled head.

This is it! I recognized the track rising up through a natural meadow into a cluster of aspens. I glimpsed the top of the rusted water tower beyond the ridge.

So I got out of the car and followed the path, sending the deer bounding away. I came to the trees, whose leaves rustled in the breeze. It reminded me of a million wings beating.

I had to stop before I reached the ridge and take a deep breath. Then I steeled myself to walk on.

The leaves rustled louder than before, though they were still a long way off and I was walking through long silvery grass. Then I struck away from the track, taking the shortest route to the top of the hill and resting again in the shadow of the water tower. Now the land sloped away, down into a wide valley where a creek ran.

At first I didn't see the house. And I was already telling myself how crazy I was to have imagined all that, how grief could play weird tricks, like it was the mind's way of kicking you when you were already down.

I was ready to give up when I heard a door banging and I spotted the broken-down barn.

My heart pounded.

Bang—again! And the rustling leaves still reminded me of flapping wings, filling my ears with an immense sound. So I stumbled from the shadow of the water tower, down the slope toward the barn.

But I'd only gotten halfway down the slope when I saw two figures working in the overgrown meadow—a couple of guys fixing a gap in an old razor-wire fence. It was such an everyday sight that I forgot to be afraid, until the younger of the two glanced up and I recognized him.

"Jonas!" My voice came out strangled and hoarse. I stopped on the hillside and gazed at his tall, skinny outline.

Jonas Jonson had ridden his Harley on a straight road

out of Centennial with Zoey riding behind him. He crashed and died but there was scarcely a mark on him. Zoey spent six weeks in a coma and still doesn't remember what happened.

Jonas saw me and turned to the older man—the gray-haired guy they called Hunter who had closed the barn door on my first visit. Immediately, Hunter put down the tools he'd been working with and made a beeline up the hill toward me.

I could hardly breathe. I wanted to run but I didn't know which way to turn.

Hunter kept on coming at me—a tall figure with gray, flowing hair, dressed in a dark shirt, his face pale and expressionless. I saw Jonas in the background shaking his head at me and warning me off.

I raised my arms in surrender. "Look," I said to Hunter, "I don't know who you are or what's happening, but just back off, OK?"

He stopped around ten paces away. His dark eyes glared.

"I came to find Phoenix," I explained.

Other people were emerging from the willows—two girls in their twenties, one with short, red hair, the other carrying a little kid with fluffy hair the color of straw. And there was a small, wiry guy with them. They all went to stand beside Jonas.

"Phoenix," I said to Hunter in my desperate, strangled voice. "Where is he?"

Hunter kept on staring, feet planted wide apart, hands on hips.

He didn't react. I was drawn to his gaunt face and unflickering, dark eyes.

Why was his skin so pale? Outdoors guys like him usually looked tanned and healthy after a summer working in the sun.

It was the last clear thought I had before the pounding of wings grew louder still and filled my head. Hunter stared and the wings beat, like a force field battering me back the way I'd come. A smothering sensation came over me, and then a panic. The invisible wings were all around, forcing me to fight with my fists at thin air. I punched but there was no enemy. Breathless, turning this way and that, I yelled for Jonas to help me.

Hunter didn't glance over his shoulder. He seemed to know that Jonas wouldn't move a muscle.

"Phoenix, where are you?" I cried. He loved me. He would save me.

But whatever Hunter was doing was stronger than any plea I could deliver. He was staring at me and making the million wings beat louder, forcing me back to the water tower, sending me reeling into its shadow.

"Where am I?" I gasped. I crouched and put my hands over my head to shield it. "Please, someone, tell me what's happening!"

I was down on the ground, in deep shadow, and suddenly a shape loomed over me, a face came close to me with eyes as dark as death. A skull face that shifted and dissolved and didn't seem to be attached to a body. And then another came at me, worse than any nightmare, so close that my heart almost stopped and I screamed—again and again.

Here's a question for an ethics major in search of a project: Who invented funerals and why? I mean, what sense do they make?

Six guys from our class carried Phoenix's coffin down the aisle. Logan was one of them. Phoenix's mom, Sharon Rohr, stood next to Brandon, with his little brother, Zak, on her left. Zak wore a black tie and a stiff white collar that wouldn't lie flat. The Rohrs were dry-eyed while the whole church wept.

"You OK?" Hannah whispered to me a hundred times.

I nodded and stared at the cross on the altar, trying not to hear the wings or see the two skull faces lunge at me then dissolve.

"Ashes to ashes," the pastor chanted at the graveside.

Mrs. Rohr threw a single red rose onto the lowered coffin. Brandon stood with an arm around Zak's shoulder.

The wings sounded loudly in my ears. The day was still and blue, and it didn't feel as if I was saying good-bye.

"OK?" Hannah and Jordan checked with me again.

I nodded. The churchyard backed up against a steep hillside where a dozen or more of Brandon's friends had gathered to watch the ceremony. They were perched on the rocks, dressed in jeans and T-shirts, mourning Phoenix in their own way.

"Look!" I gasped, and pointed to a high, flat rock. Phoenix was standing there, gazing down on us, looking serious for once.

"What? I don't see anything." Jordan shook her head sadly, took my trembling hand, and lowered it to my side. Hannah put her arm around me and led me away from the graveside.

As soon as I could, I left the official wake. I went home to change out of my black shirt and pants into a patterned summer smock and jeans that I knew Phoenix liked.

For once Jim was home, talking at the kitchen table with Laura.

"You didn't stay long at the funeral," Laura said, interrupting me en route to the front door.

"So? You didn't even go."

"Four in one year," she said, shaking her head. "It's too many."

"The Madisons went. So did the Jonsons." For some reason I wanted Laura and Jim to feel bad.

"Well, your mom isn't good friends with the Rohrs," Jim pointed out. "They only came to live in Ellerton a year ago."

"Just before all this started." Laura sighed. She pushed a newspaper across the table toward me. "Did you know they finally recorded a verdict at Jonas's inquest?"

I picked up the paper and read the headline. "First Teen Fatality: Death Rider Traveling at 90 mph."

The rush of wings grew louder again. I saw Jonas as he'd been yesterday, bending over the fence, twisting two ends of razor wire together.

"Was the Bishop family at Phoenix's funeral?" Jim asked.

I shrugged. *Wings, please stop. Ghosts, stop messing with my head.*

"I guess not," Laura decided. "They only brought Zoey out of the hospital on Saturday. They would want to stay home and take care of her."

Zoey: Jonas's passenger—and my ex-best friend—who'd had four surgeries since the accident. This time the doctors hoped she would walk again.

"Imagine how they must feel about the dangerous driving verdict." Jim had to state the obvious, as usual. "If Jonas hadn't been on a speed trip, this never would've happened to their daughter."

"And I've known the Bishops forever," Laura said. "They're such good people."

I felt the unspoken contrast and it blew a fuse in my brain. "Meaning the Rohrs aren't good people? Meaning, they have a son with a criminal record and no one wanted them to move here, not when they heard that Brandon had been to jail."

"Your mom didn't say that," Jim pointed out. He took the newspaper, folded it, and stacked it in the magazine rack.

"She doesn't have to say it," I accused. "She didn't come clean and admit she didn't ever want me to date Phoenix, but it was totally obvious. She's probably even glad that he's dead!"

"Darina!" Laura stood up in protest. "That's not true. I wouldn't want this to happen to anyone. I feel so sorry for you…"

"All we're saying is you need to get a hold of yourself." Jim stepped in, and this was a big mistake. If he'd left Laura and me to talk it through, we might have been OK.

"As in: 'Don't play the drama queen'?" I yelled. "As in: 'Remember you only dated the guy for a couple of months. Get over it, why don't you?'"

"No, Darina." Laura tried to get near me.

"You're putting words into her mouth," Jim complained.

I groaned and shook my head. What was the use? "I'm out of here," I said.

As I drove out to Deer Creek, the sun was high in the sky, baking the pink granite boulders to either side of the narrow road. A red kite soared on a wind current way overhead.

Music for a dead friend—I could hear it from half a mile away, bouncing off those rocks beside the clear running water. Loud and metallic, banging to a heavy beat—Brandon's taste, not Phoenix's. So much so that I almost turned back.

But other cars were coming up behind me. Kids revved their engines and leaned out of the windows, yelling for me to head on. "Let's party!" "Drive, Darina, drive!"

"This is so what Phoenix would want." Some girls from our senior year at Ellerton High were sitting by the creek as I drew up and got out of my car. Water dripped from their clothes and hair, as if they'd swum fully dressed. "He wouldn't be into black and all that grieving," someone agreed. "He'd want us to have fun."

How do you know? Did you ever even talk to him? I walked right on past and went to say hi to Brandon.

"You came," he muttered, half raising his eyebrow. He'd taken off the funeral jacket he'd bought at Laura's store and loosened his tie. His eyes looked heavy, as if he hadn't slept in a week.

I nodded. "This is unreal," I said, glancing around at kids dancing in the open air. They acted like they always did—guys laid-back and cool, girls glitzy and flirty. Did it feel right? I was too unsettled to know.

"It's the way we say good-bye." Brandon dipped into a big cooler and took out a can. He handed it to me. "Enjoy," he muttered, sliding off to talk to some guys from one of the cars that had followed me up the track.

The music thumped at my head as I went to sit on a rock overlooking the creek. I stared down into the clear water there for maybe ten minutes before Brandon came back and perched on the rock beside me.

"So, Darina?"

"So?"

"How are you doing?"

"Not good," I confessed. "How's your mom?"

"Not good either. It'll take her awhile." He stared at the fast current. "She emailed Dad about what happened to Phoenix, but he didn't reply."

"Where's your dad living?" I knew from Phoenix that the Rohrs had split just after Zak was born and that there'd been zero contact since.

"Europe somewhere. Germany, I guess. Maybe he changed his address. Anyhow, Mom never thought he'd make it to the funeral."

"That's sad," I murmured.

"So what's new?" Brandon stood up to toss his empty

can into a trash bag then changed the subject. "You haven't danced?"

I shook my head.

"Or been in the water." Brandon clearly didn't want me sitting there looking tragic and casting a cloud over the party.

"Swimming I can probably do," I conceded. The thought of jumping in and having the cold, deep water close over my head suddenly seduced me, so I stood up, teetered at the edge of the rock, then took a great leap.

The cold shock of the water hit. I sank to the bottom and felt the current swirl around me, opened my eyes in the watery world of weeds and smooth rocks. For a few seconds I was weightless, drifting, rolling with the current. Then I pushed off from the bed of the creek and rose to the surface.

I broke clear with a gasp and sucked in air, realizing that the water was rapidly carrying me downstream and that I hadn't worked out an exit strategy.

"Swim, Darina!" Jordan yelled from the bank. "For God's sake, swim!"

She was there with Logan and Hannah in an out-of-the-way place under some trees. I was being carried fast between the sheer rocks.

I kicked hard against the current, just enough to stay level with Jordan and Hannah while Logan quickly threw off his shoes. But before he could act, I saw Brandon leap from rock to rock along the bank then dive in. He was downstream of me and I was losing strength, sliding toward Brandon, taking in gulps of water as I was sucked toward a massive boulder in midstream. I went under, down into the shadowy depths.

As I gave into the tugging current, Brandon's arm locked around my waist. He dragged me to the surface and swam strongly toward the weird boulder, hoisting me onto its dished surface then scrambling up after me.

And there we were, me rescued from a near drowning, both stranded in the middle of the creek, crouching in the hollow of the scooped-out rock like two pygmies resting in the palm of a giant's hand.

I only went into therapy to keep Laura quiet.

It was two days after Phoenix's funeral and I still hadn't slept. I wasn't eating either, and she'd convinced herself that my incident at Deer Creek had been a secret cry for help.

"Why did you have to tell her?" I'd asked Logan. He'd come around to my house the next day and I hadn't wanted to talk to him. So he'd sat at the table with Laura and Jim instead, and they'd squeezed the whole story out of him—my plunge into the water, the way the current had caught hold of me, and how Brandon had played the hero.

How the rest of the gang had taken a rope from one of their trucks and slung it across to the rock.

"I don't like the guy, don't get me wrong," Logan had said to my folks. "But Brandon definitely saved Darina. And it was him who came up with the idea of the rope. They used it to pull her onto the bank."

"My God, she's suicidal!" Laura whispered to Jim that night after they went to bed. I could hear plainly through the paper-thin wall.

"It's worse than I thought," he agreed.

Next morning they got me an appointment with the local shrink.

Her name was Kim Reiss. I went in at two thirty, gritting my teeth and knowing I wouldn't like her.

"Hey, Darina, take a seat," she began. No psychiatrist's couch, no big desk, no notebook. The room was light and plain: two comfy chairs, facing each other. The shrink had a quiet smile, high cheekbones, and a cute haircut. There was an inch-long scar down one cheek and I wondered about that. "Let me tell you about the method I use and see if you're comfortable with it," she went on.

I sat down and stared out of the window, emphasizing that I wasn't interested. *I don't even want to be here,* I said with my whole body.

"We use something called cognitive therapy," Kim

explained. "No deep psychoanalysis—we just focus in on what's troubling you right now, this minute, and we work out practical strategies to handle it. Really simple, I promise."

I glanced at her. "My boyfriend got killed," I said in a flat voice. Then I looked quickly out of the window again before she could make eye contact. *Chew on that, why don't you?* my body said.

She didn't react. She waited.

"He got killed, but I still see him."

"What was his name?"

"Phoenix Rohr. He was in a fight. I was waiting for him out at Deer Creek, but he didn't show up." Why was I saying all this? I'd gone in there because Laura had prepaid for the session, period. "There was blood on the ground. He didn't call me."

Kim was watching me, still waiting.

"Don't say you're sorry," I warned. "I'm sorry. *You're* sorry. Everyone's sorry."

"But you see him?" It was her second question, right on target.

"You think I mean in my dreams, don't you? People dream about the ones they've lost. I know that."

"Not in your dreams?" Kim prompted.

"When I'm awake," I insisted. "Awake as I am now. I see

35

them all: Jonas, Arizona, Summer, and Phoenix. They're really alive and beautiful. Not corpses."

"Ghosts?" she asked.

I shook my head. "More solid. More real. They smile and talk. Scary Hunter takes care of them. They're the Beautiful Dead."

Kim's gaze didn't waver. She didn't seem to think I was nuts. "You loved Phoenix?" she asked gently.

"Totally. I can't tell you." *He saw into my heart, I saw into his. Our guards were down, right from the first kiss. We were completely open.*

"You're lost without him?"

As I nodded, the tears spilled down my cheeks.

"Words don't cover grief," Kim agreed. "We don't have the vocabulary to express it fully. And what you're experiencing is common—seeing Phoenix in the places you always saw him, as if he's still here."

"What about places we never went?" I had in mind the old barn at Foxton, but I wasn't ready to spill the beans about that.

"That too," she said. "Phoenix fills your head right now. He can pop up wherever you happen to be."

"And it seems totally real?" I checked. Maybe this was it after all—I was hallucinating like crazy because I was so grief-stricken. Not quite crazy, but drowning in sorrow.

"Trauma is a tricky customer," my new shrink explained. I was liking her after all. She wouldn't need to hear about my relationship with Laura, or pry where she wasn't welcome. "And it's not unhealthy for you to be remembering Phoenix so vividly, so soon after his death."

"Thanks." I fell silent then. *What about Jonas, Arizona, and Summer?* I wanted to ask. *What about the sound of wings inside my head, the skull faces and Hunter giving me a look that could kill?*

"So I suggest you don't stress too much about it, and meanwhile we talk in detail about how you should take care of yourself."

No pressure from my calm counselor then. I was grateful. I took a deep breath and dried my tears. We talked for a long time about rebuilding a pattern of healthy eating and sleeping, agreeing that I should come back in a week.

"Don't be too hard on yourself, Darina," Kim advised as I got up to leave. "Remember you're human."

"Meaning?"

"Be ready to share. Expect to break down and ask for help. There's a whole lot of support out there."

I blinked then nodded.

"Good. See you next Thursday. Make it four thirty."

Out in the waiting room, I almost walked right past Zoey in her wheelchair.

"Why are you here?" I challenged when I spotted her. I didn't mean it to sound so unfriendly.

"Same question," she shot back. "Are you going crazy like everyone else?"

I hadn't seen Zoey in almost a year. She looked totally different—much skinnier, and her blond hair had grown out to its natural brown. Then of course there was the wheelchair, plus the scared look in her dark eyes.

"No, I'm cool," I lied. "How's it going with you?"

Zoey shrugged. "They put steel plates in my legs. They fused my spine in two places so I can stand. I'm good."

It was so bad we smiled. "Zoey, I'm sor—"

"Don't say it!"

"OK." There was a long gap then we both spoke. "I came to visit," I told her.

"I heard about Phoenix," she said.

"Lots of times," I ignored her and rushed ahead. "After the accident, I came to the hospital. All the weeks you were in the coma I came to sit with you."

Zoey frowned. "They didn't tell me."

"Then afterward, when you woke up, your dad wouldn't let me come. He said you were too sick to have visitors."

"Listen—I don't remember anything. I mean, really—nothing!"

I was shocked. "But you know me?" I checked.

"Sure, Darina. I remember the time before and most things since the crash. But right there, where the accident happened, there's a black hole. That's why I'm here—for PTSD."

Post-traumatic stress disorder. The thing that soldiers in war zones suffer from. It's a neat label for crazy, violent stuff going on in the head.

"Me too, I guess." I almost told Zoey that I'd spotted Jonas mending a fence out at Foxton, but that would have been too stupid.

"So will you start to visit again?" Zoey asked. She gave me a pleading look.

"If your folks will let me."

"Pay no attention to what they say. Definitely come," she said, pressing a button and steering her chair toward Kim's opening door. "Talk to me about what happened, Darina. Help me to remember."

That night I had the same dream/nightmare/vision—call it what you like. I was deep asleep, fighting to stay there, but the death faces rushed at me, with their black eye sockets and yellow-white skulls. They whirled close and I shuddered awake. I sat in the darkness, listening to the storm of beating wings.

Early the next morning I drove out to Foxton like a person possessed.

I gripped the steering wheel and hunched over it, willing my crappy car to go faster up the hills, taking sharp bends with a squeal of tires, throwing up a spray of dirt as I left the paved road behind.

I dumped the car by the stand of aspens and ran through the long grass toward the ridge. There was the tall water tower and the slope down to the house and barn. The rusted truck was still parked by the house and then the barn door banged shut.

Stay away! said the wings in my head, like a huge flock of birds rising into the sky. Beyond crazy, I ignored them and ran down the hill past the recently mended fence toward the barn.

At any moment I expected to see Hunter. He would stride out of the house and glare at me, send the skull heads rushing at me, scaring me half to death. Or he would be in the barn with the others—the women with the child, the young guy, and my fellow students from Ellerton High.

But no one interrupted me as I slowed down by the house, which seemed empty, its windows grimy, paint flaking from the frames. The pale green door was firmly closed.

I crept toward the door and turned the handle. It was locked. *Stay away! Don't come near!*

I peered through the nearest window and saw an old kitchen range and a bare table. A row of green and white plates was arranged on a dresser. A dusty iron kettle stood on the hob. Step through that locked door and you went back a hundred years. There was grit a century deep, a fire grate that hadn't been lit for generations.

Turning from the house, I crossed the yard and headed around the back of the barn. Down the side I noticed an old hitching rail with yellow weeds growing up around it, and at the back was a tangle of thornbushes and spiky yuccas overlooking a small meadow of that long, silvery grass.

I paused again to wonder why I'd come and if I should go on. For a start, this was not what Counselor Kim had meant by taking care of myself. I was out here alone and I hadn't told anyone where I was, living a nightmare and not sharing it. Not trusting a single soul—not even myself.

Secondly, I could be truly mixed up. Some stuff might be fact and other parts not. For instance, seeing Phoenix everywhere—in school, at his own funeral—could be part of the post-traumatic stress thing for sure. Whereas Hunter could be real. Maybe he was a recluse who owned this broken-down place and hated intruders. In which case, he would be well within his rights to throw me off his property.

But it wasn't only Phoenix. I'd also seen Summer, Arizona, and Jonas, the first time here in the barn, before Hunter had spotted me and I'd gotten the hell out. Then the second time I'd seen Jonas again.

Sure, those kids meant something to me, especially Summer. She'd been special, not just to me but to everyone who knew her. But why should they enter my head now, when it was already full of sorrow for Phoenix? Why not before, at the point when they'd died?

I'd heard them speak. And I'd seen the dazed look in Phoenix's eyes when they welcomed him into their circle, back from beyond the grave into the world of the Beautiful Dead.

Hunter had fixed it for him to come back, Summer had explained. Hunter was the boss man.

It definitely happened! I told myself. *I've seen Phoenix in this barn, surrounded by people I know are dead.*

I stepped forward through the bushes until I found a narrow door into the barn, probably used to lead horses out into the back meadow. It hung on rickety hinges, which creaked as I opened the top half and climbed inside.

The barn was dark and smelled musty, as before. A stack of hay bales had disintegrated across the dirt floor; there was an ancient swallow's nest in the eaves. The wide front door banged.

"No one's here," I muttered, feeling a thud of disappointment. The fine gossamer of spiders' webs was undisturbed, the silence felt complete. *I made it all up,* I thought.

And for a second I was relieved—almost free.

Then the door swung open and I saw the gleam of a small metal object on the floor by the wide entrance. At first I thought maybe it was part of an old horse brass that had fallen from the dusty harnesses hanging on the nearby hooks. But it seemed too shiny and new. I strode forward to pick it up, turned it between my fingers and recognized the Harley insignia stamped into the steel buckle.

I examined the Harley Davidson skull logo and the motto "Always Stay True to the Core," the biker's icon. The buckle in my hand made my heart race.

"Jonas!" I murmured. I would lay down my life that this was no coincidence and the buckle belonged to him.

It was then, as I stood in the dark barn with Jonas's buckle, that the sound of the beating wings rose again and I sensed someone outside.

I grasped the buckle tight, turned, and fled toward the stable door, wrenching at the bolt so I could stumble through. But it was rusty and I would have to climb out, and someone was entering the barn—probably Hunter on the prowl for intruders—so I grew panicky again, and clumsy, losing my balance and falling back against some broken hay bales.

Footsteps came near and a hand grasped mine to help me up. The hand held me tight.

I was looking into the face I loved.

"Sit down here," Phoenix said gently.

We sat cross-legged on the dirt floor, surrounded by hay. I held both his hands and stared into his beautiful blue-gray eyes. *So* beautiful—everything about his smooth, pale skin, his high forehead rising to thick dark hair, the lightness of his eyes, his smiling mouth. And his body—I knew the breadth of his shoulders, the strong curve of his chest like they were a part of my own self.

"You never came to Deer Creek." I said the first useless thing that came into my head.

He stroked my cheek with his thumb, a gesture I loved. "Oh, Darina, I'm sorry," he said with a sigh.

"I miss you so much. It hurts so much. More than an ache—a sharp pain."

"I would give anything for it not to have happened," he swore in a whisper, leaning forward to kiss my mouth. "I can't bear to see how hard you're hurting."

I kissed his cool lips. I breathed him in.

"Where did you go? What's happening?" I begged at last.

Phoenix kept on saying sorry and kissing me—my mouth,

my face, my neck. I stroked his smooth hair then rested my fingers on the nape of his neck.

"Tell me," I pleaded. I felt I'd stepped over an unseen brink, sensed that I was falling, though the ground beneath me was firm.

"I can't explain," he told me. "It's against the rules. In fact, I shouldn't be here now, talking to you."

"Whose rules?" I was desperate for this to make sense, for me to be able to carry on touching him and talking to him. Now that I'd found him, I wouldn't ever let him go.

"Hunter's," he replied, frowning and glancing over his shoulder. "He takes care of us. We don't get to choose how to act. He tells us."

I gazed at him a long time without speaking. Then I thanked him for breaking the no-speaking rule.

Phoenix's face relaxed into a grin. "That's what I like about us, Darina. We two never did stick to the rules, did we?"

"No," I agreed.

"That's what I always loved about you—that and your eyes. Did I ever tell you that looking into your eyes is like swimming in chocolate? I could drown in them and die happy."

"Not funny!" I protested. And too confusing. Was the Phoenix I was talking with alive or dead? "What happened to you? Can you tell me?"

He shook his head. "I only know there was a big fight. I have no clue what it was about, only that Brandon was involved so I had to go in and help. I don't know how come I got stabbed."

I grasped his hands and made him look into my eyes. "Is that why you're back—to find out exactly what happened?"

"Yeah, I was chosen."

I saw pain behind his calm words, a flickering fear in his eyes. And I was still struggling with that weird mix of emotions myself. "So, did you really die?" I whispered. *Hang on to his hands. Don't let him go.*

As he nodded, a lock of dark hair fell forward over his smooth forehead. "You've heard of limbo? It's the place where dead souls arrive—a kind of waiting room, I guess. I was there for a while then I was returned, just like Jonas and the two girls. I can tell you, it hurt like hell."

"This is so weird!" I broke in. "I'm hearing you and touching you, yet you're saying you're not alive anymore. But you're not dead either…"

"Something in between," he insisted. "Jonas, Arizona, Summer, and me—we all have unfinished business. We need to set the record straight. That's why we're here with Hunter."

"Not ghosts then?" He was too real, too flesh and blood, though he was paler than before. His eyes were clearer, as if they saw for miles.

"More solid than ghosts," Phoenix agreed. Standing up quickly, he pulled me with him then put both arms around me.

My head swam. I wanted never to move from this spot.

"Darina, I'm really here," he promised. Then, as suddenly as he'd stood up, he let go of me and started to pull his black T-shirt over his head.

"What are you doing?" I cried. The sight of his naked torso stole my breath. It was as stunningly beautiful as the guys you see in TV ads, but this was up close and personal, this was flesh and blood.

Phoenix turned his back. "Look between my shoulder blades. What do you see?"

With a gasp I lifted my hand and touched his lovely pale skin with my fingertips. There was a small black tattoo to the left of his spine, only about as big as a lapel button, in the shape of a pair of angel wings. "This wasn't here before."

"It's where the blade went in," he told me. "We all have this death mark—Arizona, Summer, Jonas, the others—even Hunter."

"What does it mean?" I asked. The design was delicate, perfect in its way. I traced my fingers over the area of skin.

"It's who we've become," Phoenix explained in that low

voice I loved. A ray of light flooded the barn as the door swung open. "I'm one of the living dead, Darina. A *revenant,* a zombie. I'm here to get some justice out of this situation and to comfort you."

3

I wasn't crazy after all. I'd followed my heart and found my love. I held him and kissed him, and nothing else mattered.

"You know this is dangerous for you?" Phoenix murmured, gazing at me as if he was the one who couldn't believe his eyes. He had one arm around my waist and was leaning away so he could see me more clearly. "We're sworn to secrecy—me, Jonas, and the others."

"Don't tell me—Hunter *makes* you swear."

Phoenix nodded. I'd guessed right. "You belong to the far side, Darina—to the living world. We have to keep you out."

"Is that what the beating wings are about, and the skull heads?" I told him how scared I'd been to come back to this place. "But, Phoenix, I didn't care," I finished. "All I cared about was finding you."

"And you did," he whispered, holding me tighter. His lips were soft against my cheek. "You're the only one who wanted it enough and was brave enough to fight through. But how do you feel about the zombie thing? Don't you want to run the hell away from me?"

I held a chunk of his hair and gave it a tug. "Enough about leaving! I'm here, and I'm not going anywhere." I couldn't have broken free from Phoenix at that moment even if I'd wanted to.

He grinned and for a while he was his old, joking, laid-back self. "Listen. It's not all serious revenge and justice stuff. From what Jonas tells me—and he's been here longer than me—I do get to kid around."

"Such as?"

"Number one, I can hypnotize you." He backed off, pointed a finger at me as if he'd gotten me in his sights—*bam!*

"Why would you want to do that?" I lunged forward and grabbed his wrist. "I already only have to take one look in your direction and I'll do anything you want me to!"

"OK, forget that." Phoenix pried my fingers from around his wrist. I could see from the glint in his eye that he was enjoying teasing me. "How about this? I can disappear whenever I like."

I clung on tight again, this time by wrapping both arms around his chest. "Don't you dare!"

"Other stuff too. Mind games. Time travel if I want."

"Wow, Superman." I couldn't really take this in, so I didn't act like I was impressed. My heart was too full of surprise and joy for that, and I was bewitched by his presence.

"Are you sure you aren't scared?" Phoenix turned down the corners of his mouth. He was still kidding with me and doing the stroking thing with his thumb. "You're hanging out with a zombie!"

And he broke free, raised both arms straight out in front of him, and set off in a stiff-legged, shambling walk around the barn so that I got a good view of his slim waist, the curve in the small of his back, the tiny angel-wing tattoo, and the bunched muscles of his broad shoulders.

"Yeah, yeah, I saw the movies." I sighed. "So where's the graveyard and the rotting corpses, the dreaded flesh-eaters?"

Phoenix stopped clomping and kidding around. "That's all just bad PR, shock horror. None of that is real. One thing the movies did get right though is that we do hang out in groups, and Hunter makes the rules. No free will. He holds the power."

"OK, I've already got that. And I know he'll get angry when he finds out about me."

"He already knows, Darina, believe me. His senses, especially his hearing, are super sharp. He can hear a leaf fall from the aspens by the water tank."

"Scary," I breathed. And I was serious.

Phoenix nodded. "There's no way he didn't hear you arrive."

"So why didn't he stop me?"

"He has his reasons. Maybe he wanted to test me, to see if I obeyed orders." Phoenix's eyes flickered, and he shrugged.

"Which you didn't," I reminded him, suddenly worried for his sake. "Is there some kind of punishment if you break the no-talking-to-outsiders rule?"

He gave another shrug, but this time not so careless. "We're all here as a big favor. A whole heap of dead souls want to come back from beyond the grave, but only a few get chosen, usually the ones with a mystery hanging over them. So I guess there's a bunch back there, each with an excellent reason to stand in my place. Hunter could blow me out and bring one of them out of limbo, no problem."

I stood for a while, eyes closed, hit by a sudden, heavy sense of dread.

"Phoenix, you shouldn't be here, talking to me," I said. "If you go now and never see me again, maybe Hunter won't punish you. I mean it, you have to leave."

As I was pushing him backward toward the big barn door, Phoenix turned and took hold of my wrists. "You think it's that easy?" he protested, his eyes sparking with anger. "You think I could just give you up? Look at me, Darina. It's me—Phoenix. Wasn't I always totally open with you? Look at me and read what's in my heart."

I saw nothing but a blaze of love there. The flames swallowed us both and I was helpless. "OK, we'll face it together," I whispered as the tears welled up. "Whatever Hunter's punishment, he'll have to do it to both of us—"

"Which is all very touching," a flat voice interrupted.

Hunter. The man himself had obviously been listening to every word. He strode into the barn with Jonas and Arizona, not so much taller, but seemingly towering over the rest of us. And me. "Even *my* heart would be moved, if I had one."

Phoenix heard Hunter's voice and gritted his teeth. He put an arm around my shoulder then turned to face him. "You won't hurt her," he said firmly. "She didn't do anything wrong."

Hunter advanced into the deep shadows at the back of the barn. His arms were folded across his broad chest, his thick gray hair tied back from his face.

"Darina didn't listen to the warnings," he pointed out. "Too bad."

"You don't scare me," I lied, and Hunter could see right through me. His smile was cold and cruel. "I'm not going to give up on Phoenix."

"You won't have any choice." Hunter came close enough for me to see the telltale angel-wing tattoo on his temple. It was more faded than the one on Phoenix's back, as if it had been there a long time.

"You don't rule *me*," I told him, feeling Phoenix's protective arm as I defied Hunter. "I'm not one of your little gang."

Hunter clearly didn't like my choice of vocabulary. His brows knitted in a deep frown and he glared more angrily than before. "OK, Miss Big-mouth, I've listened long enough. Weren't you paying attention when Phoenix warned you we can get inside your head and hypnotize you? Get this straight, Darina, I can wipe your mind clean, like a teacher in school wiping words off a whiteboard."

I gasped and turned to Phoenix.

Phoenix nodded gravely. "It's true. That's how come we can hang out here all this time without anyone knowing about us."

Jonas stepped forward to carry on the explanations. He came between me and Phoenix, his face earnest. "Darina, the Beautiful Dead need to be totally secret. We've been here almost a year, keeping that secret by using mind games, by wiping people's memory clear, by hypnosis."

"Exactly how?" I insisted, glancing from Jonas to Arizona. I felt alone and more scared than ever now that Phoenix had moved away.

"Easy," Arizona interrupted. I remembered the quick, dismissive wave of her hand, which she'd always done when she was alive, like brushing away a bug. "Not many people from the far side come by this way—it's too far away from the road, and they only walk over the ridge if they're out hunting, or maybe some young kids might be fooling around, camping out overnight. Whatever. One or two might spot the water tower and come looking."

"Then what?" I found myself staring at Arizona, searching for her death mark. I studied her face, with its long, straight nose and big dark eyes, the fine eyebrows arched and giving her a permanent, high-maintenance look, but nothing to suggest that she was a zombie.

"They might even see us working in the vegetable garden or the corral," she went on. "That's when one of us comes up behind and catches them off-guard. It just takes one special look."

"To hypnotize them and wipe their memory clean," Jonas added. He was half frowning, looking anxiously from me to Phoenix, and then to Hunter. "We get inside their heads and make them walk away, back over the ridge, into the aspens. Then we wake them up and they have no knowledge of what just happened."

"They just get the hell out," Arizona said with a slight smile. "They wake up with a sore head and a weird, uneasy feeling that something's not right. Most of them don't walk to their cars, they run."

"Don't tell me. They hear wings beating, closing in on them, starting to suffocate them. They don't know where it's coming from and it's loud enough to drive them crazy." I half laughed, knowing only too well some of the methods the group used to scare people on the far side. "Is that what you're going to do to me now?" I asked Hunter, who was way too quiet and was still glaring at me. "Erase my memory?"

"Maybe," he muttered. "Anyway, you'd thank me in the end. Life's a whole lot easier if you don't know we exist."

Taking a sharp breath, I grabbed Phoenix. "Tell him not to do it," I pleaded. "Now that I've found you again, I don't want to forget."

"Me neither," he muttered, staring intently at me. "I want to remember everything about you, everything about *us*."

Nobody spoke. I could hear my heart pounding. I wondered about *their* hearts, if they still beat inside their bodies.

"Darina, you know you're putting Phoenix between a rock and a hard place." Arizona's dry tone broke the long silence. "You're forgetting that he has no free choice here. As one of the Beautiful Dead, he has to obey Hunter, or else he gets sent back without sorting out his mess. But, on the other hand, if he's a good boy and does as Hunter tells him, he loses you forever."

"Catch-22," Jonas agreed.

"But I don't believe you could wipe all this away!" I gestured around the echoing barn then held Phoenix's head between my hands to make him focus on my face. I spoke so the others couldn't hear, or so I thought. But

I overlooked their ability to hear the fall of an aspen leaf. "How could I forget finding you here and being held by you, kissing you again?" I whispered. "How—?"

"Tell her, Phoenix," Arizona interrupted.

"Believe them," he whispered back, his voice choking. "Your memories would be gone. You'd never see me again."

I grew desperate when he said this. "But I won't tell anyone!" I cried, running to Hunter and pleading like a little kid. "I swear I won't tell a single person!"

Hunter's expression didn't change. It was the kind of face that could be carved in stone—you could almost see the sharp-edged chisel marks. "You think you won't. You can swear on your life, but there's always the chance that you'll make a mistake, let the secret out—and then we're finished."

"Literally," Arizona said. "If the far side gets to know about us, we're all gone for good."

"Without doing the job we came to do," Jonas added, taking up the story again. "Listen, Darina, I've been here almost a year, trying to get some clarity about what happened that day—the Harley, the road, the crash—but it's hard. I have no memory of it and it's driving me crazy. I can't get to Zoey either. She hardly ever comes out of her house. And time's running out for me. I don't have long."

"Zoey's doing OK," I told him. "She's had operations to

help her to walk. It's her folks—they're trying too hard to protect her."

Jonas put up his hand to shield his eyes. He rubbed his forehead with his thumb and forefinger. "I was so scared she was going to die," he confessed.

I shook my head. "I saw her for the first time just yesterday. She's skinny now. And she still uses a wheelchair. But she'll definitely make it."

Jonas took away his hand to show that there were tears in his eyes. "I was so stupid. Me and my Harley, acting all cool. I thought I was king of the road! We set out that afternoon, heading out through Centennial onto the highway. Zoey was laughing. She'd told her folks she was visiting a girlfriend and they'd fallen for the story."

"They didn't like her riding the Harley with Jonas," Arizona cut in. "They didn't like Jonas, period."

"She was holding me tight around the waist," Jonas recalled. "We got to the neon cross on Turkey Shoot Ridge. The road bends there but not too much." He lowered his voice to not much more than a whisper. "I rode around the bend and then nothing. Darkness. That's it."

"Jonas believes the accident was his fault." Arizona baldly stated the facts. "He doesn't remember the details but the autopsy showed he broke his neck and died on the spot. Plus he's convinced he almost killed the girl he loves."

"So does the whole of Ellerton," Jonas whispered. "They brought a verdict against me—you saw the headline."

Jonas seemed on the verge of tears. There was a choking feeling in my throat and I was halfway to crying myself. "Zoey doesn't blame you," I comforted him. "She doesn't seem bitter or anything."

"Darina, you've got to tell her sorry from me," he cried. "Tell her I never meant to hurt her."

Arizona, the voice of reason, stepped in again. "How can Darina tell Zoey anything after Hunter has wiped her memory? He's going to press the delete button, remember?"

"No!" Phoenix cried out. "Darina *will* keep our secret." He confronted the stern older man. "You can totally trust her."

Hunter gave a thin-lipped smile. "You'd stake your life on it, am I right? If you still had a life to lose."

"Don't joke. This is serious." As Phoenix went up to Hunter and tried to stare him down, Jonas, Summer, and Arizona grew nervous. "I mean it," he insisted. "I care more about Darina than I do about myself. I don't want you messing with her mind."

"Like I said before, very sweet and touching," Hunter stated without a trace of emotion. "But, boy, you don't even come close to changing my opinion, which is that Darina will crack under pressure. Then knowledge of the Beautiful Dead will leak out and none of us will get what we want. Rather, what we *need.*"

His calm reasoning finally got right under Phoenix's skin. "How come you're doing this?" he argued, passion firing up his voice so that it was louder than usual, almost a yell. "First you scare her half to death but you still let her get through the barriers. You let her and me meet again. Then you slam the door in our faces." He swung round to face Jonas. "Tell him he can't do this—he can't wipe Darina's memory!"

Jonas shrugged. "Nothing I can say will make any difference. It's down to Hunter."

Hunter turned his back on Phoenix and stared at me. "Don't you want to go back to Ellerton?" he asked. "Back to your family, trotting along to school and choosing colleges like any other kid?"

"I'm not like any other kid," I protested angrily. "I don't run with the pack. Tell him, Phoenix."

But his last protest seemed to have emptied him out and all he could do now was stand close and hold my hand.

"OK, so here's what I'll do," Hunter announced. "Right now I'm caught up in something important, so I won't make a decision until after I've given the problem more thought, maybe later today. Arizona, take Darina into the house and sit with her. Jonas and Phoenix, I need you to come with me."

I didn't want to leave the barn, terrified that once Phoenix was out of my sight I'd never see him again. But Arizona gave me a look. She played a zombie mind trick, zapped my resistance, and made me follow her without even looking over my shoulder. My limbs moved without me telling them to.

"Count yourself lucky," she told me, the wind catching her long hair and whipping it across her face as we crossed the yard. She took a key from her pocket and opened the door of the house.

"How come?"

"You have until later today—a few extra hours of being with Phoenix, of knowing what's happening out here. It's more than most people get."

Inside the museum-house, Arizona sat me down on a dusty rocking chair by the kitchen range. She perched on the table and stared at me. "I guess you love the guy," she muttered.

I met her gaze. "I don't care what Hunter does to me. Nothing matters except Phoenix."

"Lucky you again," Arizona sighed. "I never felt like that about anyone when I was on the far side, and now I guess I never will."

"So let me out of here." I saw what I thought was a chink in Arizona's armor. "Let me have that chance. Nobody will know if you leave the door open and let me escape. And I swear again that I won't tell a living soul."

She shook her head, casually swinging her long legs over the edge of the table. "Oh my, Darina. And I had you down as an A-grade student. A little freaky, but so straight As."

Angry, I sprang out of the chair. "And I always thought you were in love with yourself!" I flung back. "I was right!"

Another look from Arizona took the strength from my legs and I slumped back in the chair. "You're forgetting that Hunter hears every word we say," she reminded me. "He's out there with Phoenix and Jonas, on the lookout for weekend hunters. A bunch arrived at the Government Bridge campground, downstream from here. Hunter wants to make sure they don't stray in this direction. But that doesn't mean he's not listening to us."

I was so frustrated I felt hot tears sting my eyelids. "You're prisoners, all of you. How can you live like this?"

Arizona gave me a faint smile. "This isn't 'living'—not in any way that you'd understand. You have to get your head around that, Darina. Phoenix isn't alive anymore. None of us are."

"Wherever Phoenix is, whatever he is, I want to be with him," I told her. "That's what you have to get *your* head around."

Part of me wanted to leave at that moment. I'd never been Arizona's buddy. Nobody had, but then, everybody had.

We'd been in the same class since the beginning of high school but we'd never been close. She was the aloof type— more of a loner than me in a lot of ways, never opening up and letting people in. And maybe I'd been jealous—the looks, the style, the brains—Arizona had them all. It's what kept people away.

"OK, I'm not arguing," she told me. "But I'm not letting you leave either. And while we're here I get to put you straight on a couple of things."

"Go ahead." Resting my head against the hard wooden backrest, I tried to fight the pool of tears gathering behind my eyes.

"First, you hate Hunter for obvious reasons. But it's his job to keep the group safe. He's our overlord, and without him we'd be out of here without a trace. It's him you have to thank for finding Phoenix."

"Overlord?" I questioned. The word sounded unnatural coming from her lips. Hunter's power was getting scarier by the second. "How come he's in charge?"

"Listen. This isn't Hunter's first return to the far side. He's been dead a long time—almost a hundred years. If he was alive he'd be twenty years older than this ranch house, which he built with his own hands."

I sat up straight and stared at Arizona. "Did he die in this house?"

"Yeah. Someone shot him, right here." She tapped her forehead. "The bullet went clean though his brain. They never knew who did it, but it's too late for justice—the killer's dead and buried by now. But Hunter stayed in limbo. He became an overlord, ready to bring souls back to the far side and guide us in our mission. We're the sixth group he's led. There are eight of us—nine including Hunter. That's a whole bunch of restless souls he has to take care of, so it's no wonder he's kind of strict."

"Is he ever more…" I stopped to search for the right word.

"More human?" Arizona laughed. She obviously heard noises outside in the yard and went to open the door. She let Summer in, carrying a bowl of soup and some crackers that she placed carefully on the table. "Darina wants to know if Hunter ever loosens up," Arizona said.

"Hey, Darina," Summer said, ignoring the question and avoiding looking at me. "Hunter and the guys could be out there awhile. You need to eat."

I shook my head. "Do you think I can eat? Summer, I need to persuade Hunter to back down. He wants to zap my memory cells clear of you all. How do I stop him?"

"There's no way," she said softly.

Like the others, Summer looked exactly the way she had on what they called the far side. Long, soft, fair curls still framed her heart-shaped face. She wore a floaty, pale blue top that slipped off one shoulder to show a frame as delicate as a bird's.

"Hey, it's me, Darina, you're talking to," I protested. "We're the kids who went everywhere together...when..."

"When I was alive?" she cut in, looking me straight in the eyes. "I know, Darina. And it hurts that I can't help you. But you know why not."

"But I can find a way of helping *you!*" I was up on my feet, demanding Arizona's and Summer's attention. "You're here on a mission right? You all came back out of limbo to find justice."

They both frowned. Summer listened closely. Arizona's eyes narrowed, her lips curled in the trace of a mocking smirk.

"I can go back to Ellerton and play detective," I promised. "You tell me the questions you need to ask and I get you the answers."

Arizona laughed. "You and whose team of top homicide cops?"

Oh, please. Even dead, Arizona Taylor had to be the most annoying person in the whole of Ellerton High. "So maybe *you* don't want my help, but, Summer, I bet you do. Listen, I saw your dad the other day. I can call by the house whenever I like, give him and your mom any message you need me to."

Summer took a deep, deep breath. "I miss them. I feel so sorry."

"So do we all," Arizona cut in. "The whole town is traumatized. These things—knife crime, shootings—happen in big cities, not here in Ellerton. It's like an earthquake hit the place—the ground cracked open and everyone fell in."

I was shocked by the force of her words. The smirk had faded. She was right. Four kids from the local school had been struck down—and parents especially went through each day wondering who would be next.

"So what hope do you have of helping these people?" Arizona had dropped the scornful tone completely and genuinely seemed to want to know. "Or of figuring things out for Summer and me, for Jonas and Phoenix?"

I wouldn't be beaten; I wouldn't give in before I'd begun. "A better chance than you," I told her. "At least I don't have to hide."

The afternoon crawled by. I sat in the rocking chair feeling the dust of a century settle on me.

"Where are they?" I asked Arizona, who still kept guard. "What's keeping Hunter?"

She sat by the window, staring out. "There must be trouble at Government Bridge. Eve, one of the other girls, was called out to help. It's not the first time this has happened."

I wanted more information. "Tell me what you mean."

"Trouble's brewing. It's the start of the hunting season and guys with big muscles and guns are coming."

"I saw the mule deer up on the ridge," I recalled.

"They're here a lot," Arizona explained. "There's good grazing on the ridge and down in the valley. The place will be crawling with hunters before we know it."

"Too many for you to deal with?" I guessed.

She nodded. "Some of those hunter guys are developing a vigilante attitude. They suspect something weird is happening around here and they don't like it."

"The place spooks them and they don't know why," I heard myself add. I quickly got the picture—beating wings whooshing through their tough-guy heads, death faces swooping down at them and wiping their memories clean.

"Hunter thinks there's talk in the bars in town, at gas stations, and in the gun stores. Some guys are planning to get together. Maybe they're the ones out at the campsite right now."

I got up and paced the creaking boards.

"Don't worry, Phoenix can't get killed twice over," Arizona said with a grim smile. "Anyway, the guys with guns don't even see him and the others. We can stay invisible when we choose. Usually we don't think about it. No, I bet what happened is that the vigilantes split up into pairs and that some of them are still nosing around—until Hunter finally tracks them down. When he does, they'll be out of here fast."

Scared out of their wits and too macho to admit it. I thought of all the boasting and exaggerating that would be going on in the town bars tonight.

"You want to know something funny?" Arizona asked. "Jonas's dad is one of the vigilantes."

"No way!"

"Trust me, he is."

"That's so *not* funny," I spat. Poor Jonas, out there scaring his own dad half to death.

As we talked and Arizona smiled and I felt sick and angry, a figure appeared on the ridge and began to run down the hill. I recognized Phoenix the second I saw him through the window, so I turned and flung open the kitchen door.

"Quit that!" Arizona warned as I tried to dash across the yard. She ran after me, grabbed my wrist, and held it in a grip so tight it felt like a band of steel. So I called to him, watching him cover the ground with his long stride, wondering again how someone who looked so alive and strong could be dead.

Phoenix vaulted a wooden fence and ran across the yard. "It's OK, the campsite is clear. The hunters finally jumped in their Jeeps and headed back to town."

"How many?" Summer asked. She'd hurried after us out of the barn at the sound of Phoenix's footsteps.

"Ten altogether."

"Including Bob Jonson?" Arizona wanted to know.

"Yeah. It was tough on Jonas." Phoenix noticed her tight grip around my wrist. He frowned at her and she let me go. "Hunter took care of him, made sure he stayed out of Bob's way. But Jonas saw his dad in the distance, riding his bike along the Foxton road. He's bought a Harley, just like the one Jonas crashed."

No one said anything for a while. Then Phoenix took me gently by the hand.

"Come with me," he said, leading me into the barn.

We sat for a moment holding hands on some wooden steps leading to a hayloft, my heart pounding again. But as a shaft of warm sunlight fell across us, a sense of calm came over me.

"Darina," Phoenix began.

I put my finger across his lips. "Whatever it is, don't say it."

He stared into my eyes instead. His own eyes were that mesmerizing gray-blue, deep as the ocean, his brows straight, his cheekbones high, framing that luminous gaze.

I swallowed, drinking in the sunlight in the barn, the dancing dust, a white dove in the rafters. "Can you make time stand still?" I murmured.

"I haven't learned how to do that yet." He tried to smile, but his tone was serious. "Not even Hunter is that powerful. Darina, how long were we dating?"

The change of topic surprised me. Still, I came up with the answer quick as a flash. "Two months, two days, and seven hours. A lifetime."

"It went fast," he said as he studied my palm and traced my lifeline down to the base of my thumb. "I could never get you out of my mind—not for a moment. You were always there."

"Even before we kissed?"

Phoenix nodded, glanced down at the floor then up again at me from under hooded lids. "Since the day I walked into school and saw you. *Boom!* And when we got together, that didn't feel like a first kiss either. It felt like I'd spent my whole life kissing you."

I leaned forward, my cheek touching his. "I know. I know."

"That's what I need to talk to you about," he said. He pushed my hair back from my face and made me look straight at him. "I want you to promise that you will find a way to go forward without me—"

"Don't!" I pleaded. "I'm here now. I'm not going anywhere."

"Listen to me. Hunter will be here soon. I need you to promise before he gets here—don't do anything stupid."

"Like forget to go on living?" My feeble attempt to

lighten the mood ended in my voice cracking and tears leaking down my cheeks.

"Darina." Phoenix cupped the back of my head in his hands. "You have a life ahead of you. Live it for me, please."

"Or I could die and join you," I said before I could stop myself. "I'd come and find you in limbo. We'd be together again."

He shook his head. "That's not how it works. Stop—you're freaking me out."

"How do you think I feel?" I replied, my voice thick.

"We don't have much time," Phoenix insisted. "I have to make you understand. Love doesn't end just because I'm not around. It goes on. I love you. You love me—forever."

"*Where* does love go on? *How?*" I asked, desperate.

"It just does. Every time you think of me again—that's love. Every place we've been together, every drop of diamond-clear water in Deer Creek—that's love."

"It's not enough and you know it. It hurts too much. I need you with me, by my side."

His eyes didn't blink. "But I am there. My heart is there. Trust me."

I closed my eyes then opened them again. "Can you see the future?" I whispered. I wanted to know if I'd ever be happy.

"No. Only the past. I can take you to our first date, back

71

to the first time I held your hand and you said to me how it was weird, I wasn't like you'd thought I'd be."

"And you said, 'How did you think I'd be?'" I murmured, remembering it word for word. "And I jumped in like a hothead as usual and said I thought you'd be a tough guy like Brandon, and you laughed and said, 'Thanks for that!' And I said 'no offense, I didn't mean you weren't macho or anything, that honestly I thought you were cute…'"

Phoenix grinned, his eyes sparkling. "You see," he said, putting my own hand to my heart and holding it there. "That's where love is. It's never going to go away."

Which is when Hunter and Jonas came into the barn.

4

ere's the plan," Hunter said.

I looked at Jonas and saw he was almost broken by what he'd just been through——finding his dad among the vigilantes and watching the old man's mind being zapped by the Beautiful Dead. Jonas's head was down, his shoulders slumped.

"Darina," Hunter went on. "You get to go home with your brain in full working order."

Phoenix and I jumped to our feet. We stood facing Hunter, taking in the verdict.

"On two conditions," he went on. "First, you keep your mouth shut tight." Hunter's voice was harsh. His face was hard.

"That's cool. I promise I won't say a word," I whispered.

"I know that." Hunter walked up and came between me and Phoenix. He flicked me a look of total certainty then casually dropped the killer ingredient into the mix—the one I knew was coming. "Because if you break this promise I send the boy right back where he came from. And this time he can never return."

I reached for Phoenix's hand, but Hunter grabbed my arm instead.

"Second, when you get back to Ellerton you work for us."

I nodded. "I'll do whatever you want. Arizona, Summer, and me—we already discussed it."

"I'm well aware of that." He smiled. "As I recall, Darina, Arizona doubted your ability to seek out the truth. She doesn't think too highly of you, period."

"She doesn't know me," I retorted. "Anyhow, I'd say that worked both ways."

"So I'm telling you to keep any personal feelings you may have out of this," Hunter insisted. "Your job is to sideline Phoenix, Arizona, and Summer for now, and put all your focus on Jonas."

This disappointed me, but I was willing to play Hunter's game if it meant I got to spend more time with Phoenix. Of course I was. "What do you want me to find out?" I asked, the words tumbling out I was so eager. I wasn't taking time to evaluate, to understand how Hunter must have set this whole thing up from day one, letting me "see" Phoenix in all the familiar places, fixing it for me to stumble across the old house and barn, testing me out with the beating wings and the skull faces to see if I was tough enough. All I knew at that moment was that I was ready to die in order to help Phoenix and the others.

"I want you to make contact with Zoey," Hunter ordered. "Jonas has tried to get close and work out exactly what happened, but our powers weaken the farther away we are from our base here, plus there's always something in his way. It's up to you now."

"I can do that," I said. "And I can go online and read up on the court case. There'll be a heap of stuff there about what happened on the day of the crash."

"Maybe." Hunter tilted his head to scratch the stubble on the cleft of his chin. "But you won't find any eyewitness accounts, only measurements the cops made of the skid marks, photographs by the forensic team, and such."

"There were no witnesses, no one around," Jonas joined in for the first time. "What they say I did—speeding on the highway out of Centennial—it doesn't make any sense. I'd ridden that road a thousand times."

"So what happened to the bike?" I asked. "After the crash, what did they do with it?"

"The cops impounded it," Hunter said. "They took the evidence, worked out a speed before the accident, checked the tires, brakes, et cetera. It was all presented as evidence in court."

"No way was I doing the speed they said," Jonas insisted. "I never did crazy stuff when Zoey was riding with me."

"So we need her to remember," I realized. "If Zoey is the

only one who can back you up on this, that's what we need to happen."

"Exactly right," Hunter said in that flat, cold tone. "How's your friendship with Zoey, Darina? Is it better than your relationship with Arizona?"

"Zoey and I go way back," I said, without telling Hunter the complications. If he was the all-powerful overlord he would see inside my head and know about the Matt Fortune episode anyway. "So after I talk to her and get her to remember the details, how do I get the message back here to you?"

Hunter stared at me without blinking. "Jonas will be there when you need him," he promised.

"What about Phoenix?" I asked quickly. If I was selling my soul and swearing silence to Hunter, I wanted at least to snatch some time with Phoenix for myself.

Hunter stared at me so hard I had to lower my gaze.

"Phoenix, walk Darina up to the water tower," he said at last. "Say good-bye there and watch her to her car."

I breathed in sharply. "Thanks," I told him.

But he flung my gratitude back in my face. "Phoenix has a vested interest in keeping you safe," he explained. "He knows that if you get Jonas the answers he needs, you'll work your way down through Arizona and Summer until you come to him."

"That's not true. Phoenix isn't taking care of me for selfish reasons. He *loves* me." I almost yelled at Hunter, who was brushing past me and climbing the steps to the hayloft.

The overlord glanced over his shoulder, down into the bright, dancing dust-filled space. "I said to forget personal feelings."

"That's impossible. He loves me." I knew it and I wanted Hunter to admit it too. Phoenix held on to my hand, tried to pull me back. Jonas stood pale and sorrowful, alone in the shadows.

"Phoenix *did* love you—probably—whatever that means," Hunter acknowledged, both hands on the stair rails, ready to leap up the steps two at a time. "But now it's different. Love needs a heart. It needs blood coursing through the veins."

"So?" My voice broke. I turned in fear to Phoenix.

"No blood, no heart," Hunter said cruelly, disappearing from view. "If you don't believe me, listen to his chest."

I shivered as Phoenix walked me up the hill. It was true, and that was why the Beautiful Dead were so pale, why Phoenix's skin was cold to the touch. For the first time I fully realized what it really meant to come back from beyond the grave.

"Who do I believe?" I asked Phoenix, under the shade of the fluttering aspens, in the shadow of the water tower. "You or Hunter?"

He breathed in deeply, his head half turned from me. "Hunter's into power," he reminded me bitterly. "Being an overlord is how he gets his kicks. The guy's been dead a long time, remember."

"So if he wanted to shock me he did a good job," I admitted. Phoenix had let me put my ear to his chest and listen, like a condemned man waiting for the switch to be thrown. Then he'd silently taken me by the hand and walked me up the hill. Now he stood some distance away, gazing at the jagged mountains on the horizon.

"I come here a lot," he told me. "You see that rock? It's called Angel Rock because…"

"…It looks like a sideways angel," I said. I could make out the shape of the head and wings, and a full skirt, like a paper angel on a Christmas tree.

"And that smooth gray rock with the grooves running vertically? That's Twelve O'clock Rock."

"Phoenix," I whispered, slipping my hand into his. "You can stop talking."

He frowned and stared into the distance.

"It's OK," I said. "I don't care about what Hunter just told me."

We stood for a long time, holding hands. As long as he was there, I could survive.

"Really, there's no problem." My voice carried up into the

shimmering silver-green leaves above our heads. His finger-tips were cool. I looked up at him and his eyes contained the vast spaces of the mountains and rivers stretching out before us. "You love me. I know you do."

Forget the "sweet" in the lamest of clichés: "parting is such sweet sorrow." Saying good-bye sucks—end of story.

I left Phoenix on the ridge and walked to my car in a daze. I turned to look. He was standing there, totally still, watching me go. The idea of raising my hand to wave crossed my mind but I didn't follow it through.

With my head foggy and confused, I got into the hot car and started the engine. I wound down all the windows, and without looking back I drove away.

So now my priority was to call on Zoey. I glanced at my watch—it was already 6:30 p.m., but if I drove fast I could make it to her house inside an hour. Would that be too late for an unexpected visit? I pressed the gas pedal and bumped crazily down the dirt track, swinging around a bend then jamming on the brakes when I met another car head on.

The back end of my car swerved; there was the sound of grating metal and I ended up in the gutter.

The next thing I knew, Logan was reaching in through my open window and grabbing me by the shoulder.

"Darina, are you OK?" His face registered total shock.

"I'm good," I told him, pushing at the door and forcing him to stand back. I got out of the car and saw the two front wheels stuck deep in the gutter. The car was tilting at an angle of forty-five degrees. "What happened? What are you doing here, Logan?"

"I drove out to Foxton with a bunch of guys—Christian, Lucas, Matt."

"Where are they?" I expected to see a convoy of cars coming up the deserted track.

"Back at the old store. Christian's dad bought the place to fix up. He said we could stay the weekend and do some fishing."

"Lucky you," I muttered, getting ready for Logan's counteroffensive.

"More to the point, Darina, what brings *you* way out here?"

"I was driving around." I blamed my face for blushing, my voice for stammering just when I wanted to sound convincing.

"Why here?" Logan scratched his head and studied my car. "You know you bent your front fender?"

"It's a crappy old car anyway."

"You're blocking the road. I'll need to get Christian's Jeep to pull you out."

Wanting to avoid any more drama, I asked him if he could tow it himself.

"You know the size of my engine? No way. So you didn't answer my question. What brings you halfway up a mountain in your beat-up old car? You don't even have four-wheel drive."

"I needed time to think. I do that best when I'm driving."

Mister Sensible shook his head. "Does Laura know?"

"Oh, please," I groaned. "Like I'm five years old and ask my mother's permission to breathe."

"You're crazy, you know that." Logan's face darkened at my sarcasm. "What if something really bad had happened?"

"Isn't this bad enough for you?" For the first time I realized that I'd bruised my right forearm when the steering wheel had spun out of control. I rolled back my sleeve to show Logan.

"You need to see a doctor," he murmured. "Forget the car. Jump into mine and I'll drive you down to Ellerton."

"No doctors," I said abruptly. "Nothing's broken. I can move my fingers, see?"

"Forget the car anyway. You're probably in a state of shock. I'll take you to the old store."

Reluctantly I followed orders. "Honestly, Logan." I sighed as I sat beside him in his car. The passenger seat smelled musty and familiar—like fun times, just out of reach. My hands were shaking. "Why did you have to be in the wrong place at the wrong time? If I didn't know better, I'd say you were following me."

He turned his head and gave me a long look. "If I was it would only be to make sure you didn't do anything stupid."

"Meaning?"

"All this stuff with Phoenix has got to you. This last week you've been acting crazy, and that's OK, I don't blame you. But you need someone to look out for you, Darina. Believe me."

"And that person would be you?" I asked quietly.

We'd driven past the fishermen's shacks overlooking the creek and were pulling up at the one and only junction in Foxton. I noticed that the front door to the old store was open and a couple of guys were sitting in the side porch.

"I'd like it to be," Logan said, almost under his breath. Then he broke the mood and grinned. "You're crazier than a gut-shot possum. That's what my old man would say."

As Logan pulled up outside the store, a third figure joined the two others on the porch. I quickly identified the short, stocky one who'd just appeared as Christian Oldman. The curly-haired guy sitting back to front on a rickety wooden chair was Lucas Hart and the one in the leather jacket was unmistakably Matt Fortune.

"Hey, guys, look who I found!" Logan announced, leaping out of his Honda and opening the passenger door for me to step out.

Loud, clashing music from a sound system inside the house almost drowned him out until Christian went back in to turn it down.

"Hey, Darina," Lucas said. He stayed where he was, tilting the chair forward and tapping his feet.

I got no sign of recognition from Matt, but then again I didn't expect any.

"Darina wrecked her car on the dirt road," Logan informed them.

"I didn't wreck it," I protested, defying the Neanderthals on the porch to say one bad word about female drivers. "I just rearranged the front fender, that's all."

"You want to sit?" Lucas stood up and offered me the chair. "You look like you got shaken up back there."

"No, I'm cool, thanks." And ready to get out of there as soon as someone put my car back on the road. There was way too much testosterone zinging around for my liking, visible in the bare arms and muscles and the significant sideways glances. Plus there was Matt Fortune.

"Christian, we need your Jeep to pull Darina's car out of the ditch," Logan said.

"I'm on it." The school boxing champion didn't hesitate, and Matt followed him to the dusty Jeep without a word. Within ten seconds they were heading up the dirt road.

"Who wants Gatorade?" Lucas asked, getting up and

going inside without waiting for an answer. He brushed against two fishing rods propped against the wall and sent them skidding along the porch floor. Swearing harshly, he stepped over them and barged on.

"Lucas is James Bond without the women and minus the style," Logan said with a grin. "A man of action, yeah, but more Incredible Hulk."

"His style works for me," I confessed. I expected any minute to hear cups crashing and more cussing. Meanwhile, Logan was getting back to the subject I most wanted to avoid.

"Darina, I don't like you driving out here alone," he told me. "It's not safe."

"Yeah, and you sound like my dad." *Jeez!* I blushed again. Logan had been the one who was there for me when Real Dad took off for good. He and I were only twelve at the time, but I swear he was a better friend than I deserved. Moody, thin-skinned Darina could always count on level-headed, reliable Logan. We spent that whole summer avoiding our parents by cycling out to Deer Creek and swimming in Hartmann Lake.

"Sorry," I muttered. "That came out wrong."

He shrugged. "Anyway, have you heard the stories going around town?"

"What stories?"

"About the ridge above Foxton. Some guys swear there's crazy stuff going on up there. They hear voices, see figures moving around in the shadows."

"Yeah, guys who are out of their heads on booze," I argued, feeling the hair on the nape of my neck prickle. "You drink a few cans of beer and you start seeing stuff."

"What if it's more than that?" Logan went on. "They're talking about a ghost house hidden at the back of the ridge—some place no one sees, way off the track."

"So was that what you were looking for?" Trying to switch the focus, I took my chance to put pressure on Logan. "What are you suddenly, some kind of ghost buster?"

"Maybe," he said calmly. "Some people believe in ghosts. Lucas, for a start."

"My ears are burning. Who's bad-mouthing me behind my back?" Lucas came out carrying three greenish-yellow bottles of Gatorade. My stomach turned. I should have been thirsty, but I wasn't.

"You believe the stuff about ghosts up on the ridge, don't you?" Logan said.

"Yeah, I do. Actually, I saw a ghost once, when I was a little kid. I woke up in the middle of the night and there was one in my room."

"No way," I countered. "I bet it was your big sister wearing a white sheet and whoo-whooing!" *Please don't believe the rumors!* I silently pleaded. And I did what I could to make tough guy Lucas feel small.

"Anyway, what if I was out ghost busting, as you call it?" Logan demanded. "What's it to you?"

"Nothing," I said. This conversation wasn't going the way I wanted. "I'm just shocked you guys fell for the BS, that's all."

"We're not the only ones," Lucas pointed out. "It's the talk of the town right now. The older guys are planning to get together and check it out."

They already did. The words were on the tip of my tongue but I managed to stop them spilling out.

"Including Bob Jonson for one," Logan added.

My close shave with the truth made me nervous. What if I'd let the words slip out and let Logan and Lucas see that I knew more than I was saying? Then my sworn secret would really have been on the line. Already. Not good. I even thought I heard those zombie wings beating out a warning above my head.

"Darina, are you OK?" Logan asked. "You want to go inside and lie down?"

"No, I want to head home." I knew I was still trembling and tried to hide it. "Thanks, Logan, but I'll wait here on the porch."

Another sideways glance must have passed between Logan and Lucas, because Lucas set the drinks on the porch railing, got up suddenly, and said he'd walk up the track to check on Christian and Matt. Which meant I was in for an intense one-on-one talk with Logan, and I was still fighting off the sound of the wings.

"I want to help," he began.

"You have already. Honestly, Logan, I know you're there for me."

"So why are you fighting me off?" He came close, boxing me in a corner, making me uneasy. "Come on, Darina, talk to me."

"I have nothing to say except inside I'm hurting. Do you understand?"

The wings faded. I was doing my job.

Logan nodded. "Totally. And I want to help. It's OK; I know I'm repeating myself. I'm just trying to get through to you."

He was pinning me against the porch rail so that I could hardly breathe. I had to work out a way of making him back off before he leaned forward and kissed me on the lips.

"I hear you, Logan," I whispered, putting my hand on his shoulder and finding that he was shaking almost as much as me. "I'm truly grateful." And I pecked him on the cheek and ducked under his arm, out of that dangerous corner.

He sighed and leaned back against the wall, eyes closed until he heard the sound of a car rattling down the track.

"Here comes Christian," I muttered, stepping down from the porch.

The three guys showed up towing my battered car. The front fender scraped the ground as it bumped along.

"You need to get this fixed," Lucas called from behind the wheel.

I nodded. "Will it get me into town the way it is?"

"Wait." Christian got out of his Jeep and tested the fender. "This needs to come off," he decided, leaning all his weight on it and wrenching until it came away from the body of the car. "Throw this in the trunk," he told Lucas.

Meanwhile, Matt jumped down from the Jeep and strode silently into the store.

"OK, you're good to go," Christian said. "There's no problem with the front axle as far as I can see."

"Thank you, Mister Car Fixer." I grinned, trying to lighten the mood and quickly taking Lucas's place in the driver's seat. I waited until I heard the trunk lid slam shut. "And thanks, Lucas."

"Are you sure you're OK to drive?" he asked.

Logan stood back, seeming to view my kiss on the cheek as some kind of Judas betrayal. He'd obviously wanted more; he always had.

I nodded. "Thanks, Logan," I called softly. He was hurt and I hated to see it. But what could I do?

So I drove out of Foxton onto the smooth highway, past the giant neon cross that lit up the mountain at night, past the stretch of burned-out forest with its scorched, deformed pines, through the Centennial neighborhood into town.

Somehow that night I managed to smooth Laura's ruffled feathers.

"Oh my God, look at your car!" she cried. It was dusk and she was alone on the porch when I parked in the drive. "Darina, what happened? Are you OK?"

"Yeah, I'm fine. I swear." I ran up the steps and turned around on the spot. "See?"

She sat me down. "So what happened?"

"I was hanging out with Logan and a few of the guys. The clumsy klutz clipped my fender. Lucky we weren't going more than ten miles per hour." *Go easy with the truth, Darina. No point in ringing any alarm bells.*

"You don't hurt anywhere?" she asked anxiously. "Your neck? Your back?"

"Not a scratch." I hid my bruised arm beneath the sleeve of my hoodie. "Honestly, Mom, no big deal."

When I was younger, before I grew into myself, everyone said I looked like Laura. We had the same long dark hair and wide smile, the little pointy chin and cute nose. "You must be sisters," the guys always told us—the ones who flirted with her after Dad left. Not anymore. These days I cut my hair shorter and color it even darker. That, plus my smoky mascara eyes, made us look totally different.

"What about the car?" Laura asked. "Who'll pay to fix it? Logan's dad doesn't have any spare cash—I know that for sure."

Yeah, Laura, always thinking money, money, money. Anyway, this was easier to deal with than her fussing about my health and safety.

"I'll talk to Christian. He knows about cars. Maybe he can fix it for free."

She nodded then took out a cigarette.

"You need to quit," I muttered, making my way through the front door. "Where's Jim?"

"Out," she said. The small red point of light from her cigarette glowed like a stoplight in the encroaching darkness. Our chat was over.

There's a gap as deep as a canyon between how you come across to people and the way you are on the inside. And you feel that gap especially when you're lying in bed, not sleeping, staring up at the ceiling.

I mean, I came down from that ridge looking like the old Darina—cool, together, a girl with an edge.

Inside I was wrecked and scared as hell. I'd been with

the undead, for Christ's sake, and I was in love with one of them. Desperately, hopelessly in love.

The dark ceiling seemed to press down on me, the walls crowded in. I'd lost Phoenix and found him. I'd been falling into a deep pit and he'd caught me, raised me up, and held me in his arms again.

But my new world was full of the stuff nightmares are made of. Of all-powerful Hunter with his gray hair and steely eyes, of still-hard-to-like Arizona, gentle easy-to-love Summer, and sad, damaged Jonas…these Beautiful Dead who had been to limbo and back. They had no hearts.

I lay in the darkness, remembering Phoenix's lovely face. "I wish you would come to me," I whispered. I knew he could do that—appear and dissolve at will. "Be here when I need you."

But I only heard the distant wings, like a sigh in the air. A reminder.

"Hi, Mr. Bishop, it's Darina." Early the next morning I spoke into the intercom at the gate to Zoey's house.

"Darina?"

"Yeah. I thought I'd drop by to see Zoey." Who was I fooling? I'd tied myself in knots wondering whether to call in advance or arrive unannounced. Or should I have texted? I'd tried Zoey's cell phone but her number had been changed. I'd driven around the block five times before I'd gathered the courage to ring the bell.

"Wait there," Mr. Bishop told me.

I stood at the end of the Bishops' long, pink-paved drive, looking up at their impressive piece of real estate. The brick built house had white pillars and a colonial-style entrance. It had balconies with iron railings and a stable block to one side of the yard where Zoey kept her horses.

Her dad drove a golf buggy from the yard down to the gate. He stepped out looking like he'd just come from a country club, which was what his estate reminded me of.

"Darina," he said, as if he'd only just linked the name to the face. Either he was having a senior moment or this was a deliberate move to distance me. "We haven't seen you in quite a while."

"I bumped into Zoey the other day. She said to call."

Mr. Bishop frowned, plainly taking in my crappy car minus its fender then equally plainly disapproving of me—the hair, the makeup, everything. "Where would that have been? Your bumping into Zoey, I mean."

"In the waiting room at Kim Reiss's place." I almost saw Mr. Bishop's teeth set on edge, as if "Kim Reiss" was a dirty word with him.

"Right. Zoey doesn't go out a whole lot. Only to see her surgeons."

And her shrink, I thought but didn't say. "I promised I'd visit," I insisted.

He stood firm behind the closed gate. "Another time, maybe."

"As soon as I could."

"She can't take visitors right now."

"I thought Saturday would be good."

We talked fast and at cross-purposes until Zoey's mom appeared in the main doorway. She walked quickly down the drive.

"Hey, Darina." Her greeting was flat, but a half degree warmer than her husband's had been. "Zoey's at the window. She heard your car."

"So she knows I'm here. Cool."

Mrs. Bishop smiled briefly. "I'm sorry about Phoenix," she told me. "I understand you and he were dating."

I nodded.

"I still can't believe it. Four young lives wasted."

"Five," Mr. Bishop contradicted bitterly. "Five, including Zoey."

His wife stepped in front of him and unlocked the gate. "You'd better come in," she told me. Mr. Bishop didn't bother to put up a fight.

It wasn't as if Zoey and I jumped right back in where we'd

left off over a year ago. Too much had happened and too much had been forgotten. Talking to her was the same as watching disjointed clips from an old video recording, in no particular order and with big, big gaps.

She was sitting in her wheelchair, looking small, in a sitting room the size of a tennis court. The decorator had been given free rein on the antiques, especially the Turkish rugs, chandeliers, and the old grandfather clock.

"Wow," I said. "I never came in this room before." It wasn't wow as in *cool,* but wow as in *holy crap.*

"We switched things around," Zoey explained defensively, knowing the house I lived in with Laura and Jim was one up from a trailer, but only just. "I have a bedroom through there, with a bathroom—all on one level. And there's a ramp outside the French windows, down into the yard."

"You want to go outside?" Away from the ticking clock and the decorator's taste in red and gold striped wallpaper.

Zoey nodded. She whizzed her chair over to the windows and lifted the latch.

"I kept the horses—Pepper and Merlin. Come and see."

I'm OK with horses, so I went along to the stable block and said nice things about a couple of roan Arabians standing in their stalls.

Zoey dug out some pieces of mint candy and fed them to

the horses. "I know. I spoil them. Dad wanted to sell them, but I said no way."

"How's the walking coming along?" I asked.

"Slowly. I worked with the physical therapist yesterday and took two steps. Hallelujah!"

I laughed. "That's good." We both pussyfooted around our main topic of Jonas and the crash.

"Two steps and it hurt like hell," Zoey confessed.

"You'll keep at it. It'll get better."

"I'm seeing Kim again—Thursday, three thirty."

"Me too. Four thirty."

"I really like her."

"Yeah, she's cool."

"Why are you seeing her? Tell me again."

"Laura thinks I went crazy over losing Phoenix," I said then laughed again—a little too loudly. "So anyway, I guess you're seeing Kim to help get your memory back?"

Zoey shrugged. "It's Mom's idea. I don't really care. Nothing's going to bring Jonas back."

A shiver ran down my spine as I thought of him out at Foxton. All of a sudden I remembered I had his Harley buckle safe in the pocket of my jeans.

"You can never go back," she went on in a tired voice. "Everyone says it doesn't matter—look forward not back. Except Kim. She says it's important for me to remember."

"To fill in the blanks." I nodded eagerly. "You said you needed my help."

"Can you imagine what it's like, this PTSD? It's like knitting when you drop a stitch and everything unravels. You end up with a stupid hole that just keeps on getting bigger."

"Scary."

"Unbelievable. The hole's grown big enough for me to fall down and disappear, I swear."

Oh, the falling thing, I almost agreed. You fall and fall and the sides of the dark hole are smooth and there's nothing to hang on to, and there's no bottom either. It's how I felt when Phoenix died. "Go back to before the crash," I told Zoey without sharing. It was still too much; I was worried I'd blurt out the truth. "You remember how you and Jonas were together?"

"I loved him," she answered quietly, while the two horses stretched their necks over the stable door and demanded more candy. "How could anybody not?"

"A sweet, sweet guy," I agreed, avoiding the *he was* or *he is* dilemma.

Zoey paused and seemed to slip down one of those holes in her memory.

I waited for her to climb back up.

"I guess I have to thank you," she said after a long while.

"How come?"

"For snatching Matt away from me and leaving Jonas to pick up the pieces."

"Hold it." This was the Matt Fortune thing raising its ugly head. "I didn't 'snatch' him. The way I remember it, Matt made a sprint in my direction and broke the Olympic record to get to me." *Good-bye, Zoey. Hello, Darina.*

"Yeah, I believe you," Zoey said. But she never had and still didn't. She was convinced her breakup with Matt was all my idea. "How long is it now?"

"Almost a year and a half. I didn't handle it well, but I didn't steal Matt, I swear. He's not my type."

"Whatever." She obviously hated to talk about it. "Let's go in."

I took hold of the back of her chair and turned it in my direction. "Zoey, I would never do that. I don't play around and steal guys from my girlfriends, whatever Matt Fortune told you. In fact, when he made a pass at me that time at Hannah's party, I turned him down."

"That's not what Hannah told me." Zoey had met my gaze with tears in her eyes. "She said you grabbed Matt with both hands."

"Yeah, with friends like Hannah..." I trailed off. "After that it took me more than a year to get around to dating another guy. That's what a fast worker I am."

"Phoenix," Zoey whispered. "Jonas liked him from the

get-go. Personally, I was always a little scared of him. He was too distant."

I shook my head. "Phoenix wouldn't hurt anyone."

"But it wasn't exactly love at first sight for you two," Zoey reminded me. "When he first came to Ellerton, I heard you tell Logan you thought Phoenix was oh-so-vain. You were pretty outspoken about that."

"Shy was what he was, actually. It came across as arrogance and personally I can relate to that. But, Zoey, this is important. You do remember the Rohrs coming to town?"

"Yes. Brandon Rohr couldn't get a job. He hung out at the Harley salesroom with Charlie Fortune. I met Brandon when Jonas went in to get his bike fixed."

"That would only be a couple of weeks before your crash," I told her, growing more excited. "Can you remember anything else that happened around that time, or a little later?"

"Charlie fixed the brakes on the bike. Jonas took me out to the lake the next day."

"Not the day of the crash?" I checked.

"No. Before that."

"And there was nothing wrong with the bike?" I'd begun to wonder if Charlie Fortune had messed up—had maybe done a bad job and caused Jonas's brakes to fail.

Zoey shook her head. "We cruised out to Hartmann, no problem. It was a perfect day."

I stood in silence, giving Zoey time to recall what must now seem like her version of paradise.

"Jonas told me he loved me," she confided. "The one and only time. We were sitting on the jetty with our feet in the cool water. The sun was real hot."

Piece by piece her jigsaw was slotting back together.

"I never told anyone," Zoey whispered when I didn't respond. "Just in case it wasn't true."

"It was," I said. "He did love you."

She dragged herself back to the present, looking up at me for more, but I'd already overstepped the mark. I'd hear the wings and Hunter would be on my back if I didn't take more care.

"I could tell by the way he looked at you," I stammered. This and a couple of other pulp fiction clichés.

"Whatever." She sighed again, giving up on me and turning her chair toward the house. She saw her mom waiting by the French doors. "I'm tired, Darina. I've got to go."

"Cool. I'll come again…you know, if that's cool." *Don't go!* I screamed to myself. *We didn't get to the main topic yet.*

Zoey didn't look over her shoulder as she crossed the yard. "Thanks for coming. Take care."

Shoot! What should I do? Run after her and say I really needed her to remember about the crash, that I wanted to help her clear Jonas's name? It sounded OK in theory, but one look at Zoey's pale, defeated face told me no. Anyway, Mrs. Bishop was coming out to meet her. She gave me a wave, polite but firm.

I scooted around the side of the house, crossed the smooth lawn, and made for the gate.

"Here, let me." Mr. Bishop had hurried out of the front of the house to press buttons on the security panel. "I hope your visit didn't exhaust Zoey," he said.

"We talked," I told him. "It was cool."

"Did she tell you she took her first steps?"

I nodded.

"A miracle. If you'd seen her in the hospital even three months ago, you'd never believe that she could come so far."

"That's good news, Mr. Bishop." I was super-polite, in spite of the fact that I hated the sight of him in his yellow golfing sweater and checked pants. His dark expression told me that he felt exactly the same toward me.

"We're looking forward now," he insisted, opening the gate and waiting for me to step through. "We're focusing on the future, Darina, not the past."

With a shock I saw Jonas standing beneath a maple tree a hundred yards down the road, waiting for me to come out.

The past won't go away just because you want it to, I

almost felt like telling him. It flies back at you, like it or not. But instead I just told him good-bye.

Anyone looking at Jonas under that tree would think one of two things. Either he was a kid with problems who needed help, or he was someone you should avoid. Sick or dangerous, depending on where you were coming from. Or both. No one normal looked that pale and troubled.

"So?" he asked me as I drove my car alongside the tree.

"I saw Zoey," I said, and my voice caught. "We talked."

"How is she?" His blue eyes, set deep in their sockets, pleaded for good news.

"She's definitely doing OK. She has everything she needs."

Jonas wasn't through with questions. "Is she going to make it? I mean, will she get back to school, go to college and stuff?"

"As in, did she have brain damage after the crash?" Come to think about it, Zoey had been in a coma for six weeks with God knows what injuries.

"Yeah." He nodded, turning his head away as he waited for my answer.

For the first time I saw the small angel-wing tattoo on the left side of his neck, just below his ear and half hidden by his blond hair. My heart missed its beat and I wanted to cry. Instead I tried to comfort him. "I'm no expert, Jonas, but she seemed the same old Zoey, except for this big hole in her memory."

He kept on nodding. "The same in what way?"

I struggled to pin it down. "She still loves those two horses like they were her babies. She gives her folks way too much respect." I smirked. "So what's changed?"

"Yeah, Zoey usually conformed," Jonas agreed with a wry smile. He ran his fingers through his hair, letting his hand rest over the death mark on his neck. "And did she say anything about me?"

I was more than happy to relay that part of my conversation. "She said she loved you."

Closing his eyes and taking a deep breath, some of the weight seemed to lift from his shoulders. "She doesn't hate me?"

"Far from it. She told me about the day you two rode out to the lake and you said you loved her. She said it was perfect."

"She doesn't hate me," he repeated in a whisper.

At that moment a car drove by and broke the mood. I glanced over my shoulder and realized my own car was sticking way out in the road and that I had to move it.

"How long can you stay?" I asked him. "Will you wait while I park my car?"

"I can't stay long. Hunter wants us all at the ranch by midday. He thinks there'll be more trouble."

"OK, get in. Best to move on to a quieter place."

We drove out of town to a parking spot where no one would see us; a viewpoint overlooking Hartmann where we saw the lake glittering in the distance. Jonas seemed happy to sit for a while, just looking, and while he gazed I stole the chance to study him from close quarters.

Until the crash I'd pegged Jonas Jonson as one lucky person—even blessed. He had the movie-star looks for a start, with his big blue eyes and fair hair, a straight nose, and high forehead that made him seem smart and not just cute, lips that any girl would want to kiss. Better still, he was one of life's good guys.

He'd made a point to seek me out when things fell apart at my house—the fight over the other woman, Dad leaving, Laura heading for the big breakdown. Most of the other kids hadn't found a way to sympathize, but Jonas's reaction had been simple and kind. "It sucks. I'm sorry," he'd said.

After that, we talked about most things. Not as much as me and Logan, because Jonas lived on the other side of town. But we did stuff in school together—Jonas liked to play guitar, and so did I, though we both knew we would never reach rock-god status. We loved acting in school productions and shared a loathing of Il Duce, Dr. Valenti.

And then, when he reached sixteen there was Jonas and his Harley Dyna—this monster accessory obviously made him super cool. He rode it without a helmet whenever he thought he could get away with it, his fair hair caught by the wind, his face and bare arms a golden brown. He would drive it hard up into the mountains, making that engine roar. "Look what I found," I said, trying to ignore the angel-wing tattoo. My eyes were constantly drawn toward it. I pulled the Harley buckle from my pocket and held it in the palm of my hand. "It was on the barn floor. I guess it belongs to you."

Jonas took it and turned it over, running one finger over the silver skull and the wording of the logo. "You keep it," he told me, handing it back. "A thing to remember me by."

"Why so sad?" I asked him. "We're already moving toward some answers about the crash. Zoey told me that Charlie Fortune fixed the brakes on your bike."

"That's true, he did."

"I think we should check it out."

"Maybe. But remember the cops would go over stuff like that. Bad brakes would be an obvious thing for them to look for."

I nodded. "Could they have been OK for a while after Charlie did the work, then suddenly not OK? Then OK again when the cops examined them."

"An intermittent fault?"

"That's the word—intermittent."

"You can check it with Charlie," Jonas agreed. He got out of the car suddenly and I joined him. We gazed at the lake and the mountain range beyond. "This is the first chance for me to say thanks, Darina," he murmured.

"No problem." My throat tightened.

"You're risking a lot."

"And I've got a lot to gain, remember."

Jonas turned to me. "Twelve months with Phoenix, huh?"

Weird—I skipped the mysterious time reference here and went right back into Jonas's situation. "So, after you dissolve and disappear or whatever it is you do, I'll drive over to Charlie Fortune's place, ask some questions, find out if Charlie's got something to hide."

"You take care, Darina." Jonas's warning flipped in and out of my consciousness, just like the twelve-month thing. What did it mean? And why couldn't I focus on it?

"I'll call Zoey and fix up another visit," I told him. "Each time we talk she'll fill in a few more gaps, you'll see. Before long she'll be remembering the whole day and how the crash happened."

"A week Tuesday it'll be exactly one year." He was off on his track, me on mine. "That's ten days from now."

"Listen to me, Jonas. I'm certain the key to everything lies with Zoey. If only she can remember."

"Ten days is all I have," he told me.

I stopped chasing my idea and switched to what he was saying. "After ten days what happens?"

Suddenly Jonas realized there was something important that I didn't know. He hesitated and tried to brush it off. "Let's get in the car and drive."

"No! What do you mean, ten days is all you have?"

"That's why Hunter brought you in to help," he explained slowly. "My time here is running out. It's the same for all of us. The Beautiful Dead have exactly a year to find out the truth about how we died and get justice. No extensions, no second chances."

"Then what?" I asked the question though I dreaded the answer, feeling the blood drain from my face and my hands begin to shake.

"We step aside and give someone else a chance."

"*All* of you?" I whispered, unable to take it in.

"All," Jonas confirmed. "Me, Arizona, Summer, and Phoenix. We have no free will, no choice. We leave the far side and go back beyond the grave—end of story."

With my emotions in a tailspin I drove across town to Charlie Fortune's workshop. In a crisis like this, I find myself something to do, and I'm better if it involves driving. Don't ask me why—especially since my driving had been less than stellar recently.

The workshop wasn't easy to find, so I had to ask directions. A woman in a dry-cleaning store pointed to an awning fabricator's unit on a small industrial estate. "Take a left there and you'll find Charlie's place."

I followed the instructions and pulled up outside a showroom window with a gleaming Softail motorcycle on display—a metal giant, all silver exhaust pipes and wheel guards, with a slick leather seat and high handlebars. Outside the building there were six or seven other bikes and two guys dressed in biking gear lounging against a wall. They stared hard at me and my beat-up car.

I braced myself and walked past them, through a side door into a high space stuffed with tires and spare parts. In one corner of the workroom was a small office hung with the usual calendars and a notice board with pinned lists and receipts. Sitting at the desk in the office was Matt Fortune's older brother, Charlie—a little heavier and already losing his hair. He was talking to a guy who was turned sideways—an older version of Jonas who I recognized right away as Bob Jonson.

I knew that Charlie had seen and chosen to ignore me. "So how come the Dyna got so beat up?" he asked Bob. "Where the hell did you ride it?"

"Places you don't want to know," Jonas's dad replied, looking sheepish.

"You've only had her, what is it, three months?"

"Three and a half. I had to save real hard."

"You're not treating her right. These babies need your total respect." Charlie stood up and came out into the workshop to study scratches and dents on the exhaust system of Bob's bike.

"I hit a patch of rough track," Bob explained, only half acknowledging me then stating his case to Charlie. "We were out at Foxton, by Government Bridge. I ran into trouble."

"Again?" Charlie crouched down for a closer look. "Tell me, what are you guys looking for up there?"

"Nothing. Just doing a little hunting." Bob clammed up and waited nervously for Charlie to tap a few panels and tug on some brackets.

"That's not the way I heard it." Charlie stood up straight. "I heard a bunch of you went out there on the strength of stories running around town. The ones about squatters or some such, up on Foxton Ridge."

"Maybe," Bob said grudgingly. "So?"

"So you run into trouble, but no one says exactly what kind

of trouble. And you arrive back looking like you saw something you didn't like up there. You know what I think?"

Bob folded his arms across his chest. "Go ahead, Charlie, tell me."

"It's not about squatters. This stuff with the kids, including your boy, Jonas, it's spooked everyone real bad. I've talked with Matt. I know how big a deal it is."

This is where I came in. Like it or not, the guys had to let me into their conversation. "I saw Matt up at Foxton last night," I butted in. "He was there fishing with Christian Oldman and a couple of others."

"God damn it, I told him to stay away!" Charlie reached for his cell phone but before he called Matt's number he turned to Bob again. "Foxton is trouble, right?"

"Something's definitely going on," Bob confessed. "It's not right for a bunch of guys—normal, everyday guys like me—riding out there, taking a look, doing nothing in particular, all to feel the same way."

"Which is?" Charlie demanded.

"Weird stuff. We all felt a wind, like a storm coming, but no clouds in the sky. To me it sounded like a big flock of birds gathering, kind of driving you back, not letting you go forward."

"Wings?" Charlie echoed.

I stood paralyzed, helpless to halt the conversation and

half expecting to see one of the zombie death heads materialize right in front of me.

"I know, it doesn't sound like a bunch of invisible birds would drive you away from a place. But I tell you, Charlie, I swear I saw things too. I was riding my bike up a track, over rough ground, and I saw a woman with a baby, out there in the middle of nowhere."

Charlie's eyes narrowed. "Alone?"

Bob nodded. "Then the weird stuff—shadows started moving and closing in, the wind from the wings rose again. It felt like faces were crowding in on me, so I rode the hell out of there."

I swallowed hard, wanting to stop the flow of Bob's confession but stuck for a way to do it. Luckily Charlie did it for me.

"Man, you need to see someone about this. Talk to a shrink about losing your boy. I'm sorry, Bob, but that's how I see it."

Bob shook his head. "I wasn't the only one. When we got back to town, all the guys had the same story—shadows, faces, the whole deal. We definitely need an explanation, and until we have it we're not going to rest. So now four of us plan to head back out there later today."

I wanted to protest, but Charlie shrugged off the situation and dialed his brother's number. "Just do something for me," he muttered to Bob as he waited for Matt to answer. "Next time you visit Foxton, spare the Harley and take the old Kawasaki."

"Hey, Darina, you been swimming lately?"

I froze in my tracks as I fled Charlie Fortune's workshop. This was all I needed—Brandon Rohr had joined the two guys hanging out outside. His voice followed me as I regained my composure and headed for my car. And he jokingly told his friends about my near-drowning experience in every drenched detail.

"What happened to your car?" he called to me after they'd finished laughing and clambered astride their bikes, roaring the engines and cruising off along the street. He strode toward my car.

"The fender fell off," I replied, settling into the driver's seat. "What does it look like?"

"Charlie doesn't do car repairs," Brandon told me calmly, thrusting his hand out to stay the door before I could close it. "Only bikes."

"Yeah, I just found out." *Back off, Brandon. Leave me alone.* I needed to warn Phoenix about what I'd just heard from Bob Jonson.

"So how did it happen?" he asked more seriously. "Who did you hit?"

"Logan Lavelle, actually." I was calm with Brandon, but underneath I was desperate to drive away. "He's a kid in my class. It's cool."

Brandon walked slowly around my car then kicked the dent where the missing fender should be. "This piece of crap is falling to pieces."

"Tell me about it." I closed the door and started the engine.

He stood in my way. "Phoenix didn't like you driving this old heap. He said you could use a new car."

I bit my lip, surprised that Phoenix had ever talked to his brother about me in such a way, and surprised twice over that Brandon should remember the conversation.

"He was right," Brandon grunted.

"Yeah, when I win the lotto." I eased the car forward. "Until then it's either this or I walk." Top of my list, well before any talk about a replacement vehicle, I needed to go and find Phoenix before Bob Jonson and his friends came searching again. "Step out of my way, Brandon. I have to be somewhere."

"What's the rush?" he asked, leaning in through the passenger side window. "Try driving at half the speed, why don't you? That way you won't run into stuff."

"Thanks for the road safety advice. I really need to leave now!"

He curled down the corners of his mouth—one feature that did actually remind me of Phoenix, with its full top lip and small kink that pulled it farther down on one side. "Why don't you let me ask a few people about finding you a new car?"

Drumming my fists against the steering wheel, I gave him three reasons why not off the top of my head. "Because I don't have the cash—not a cent. Because I don't have a job to pay for it month by month. Because my folks can't afford it."

"Who said anything about paying?" he drawled, still leaning in. "I know a lot of people with too many cars in the garage, just taking up space."

"Don't go out of your way to do stuff for me," I protested. Ulterior motives and unsavory thoughts about Brandon were circling around my head.

"Why not?" he asked.

"Because," I snapped.

"Not even if Phoenix asked me to?" He waited to see the shock register on my face then stood up and slammed the palm of his hand on my roof three times. "Take care how you drive, Darina," he said, waving me off.

It was only when I stopped at the traffic light in Centennial that I remembered there was more than one road through Foxton and decided not to take the highway.

It was important for me to reach the ridge without Logan and his fishing buddies seeing me, and without running into Bob Jonson and the rest. If I took the back road I would avoid them and might even get there faster.

So I swung left at the light and followed a narrow track, passing close by the giant neon cross, then looking down from Turkey Shoot Ridge to the bend where Jonas and Zoey's crash happened. There was a twist in the road between sheer, dark rocks but no major danger that I could see. I drove on, higher into the mountains into the pink light of the setting sun.

Up on the high road I came across a Jeep parked under some redwoods and two guys in checked shirts drinking beer from cans. They had rifles resting against the back of their car.

"Hey!" The guy with the beard flagged me down. "Seen any sign of elk?"

I shook my head, checking their license and feeling relieved to see that it was an out of state plate.

Most likely they knew nothing about the disturbances on Foxton Ridge.

"Seen much deer?" the second man asked.

I nodded quickly then sent them off in the direction I'd just driven. "Yeah, plenty down by Turkey Shoot."

"How many?"

"Ten, eleven maybe. On a meadow behind the ridge." It was a lie. I'd seen no such thing. But I liked the graceful, big-eyed mule deer better than the big-bellied, redneck hunters.

They thanked me, swallowed down the rest of their beer, tossed away their cans, and threw their guns in the back of their Jeep.

Satisfied, I drove on up the mountain, seeing no one else until I reached the end of the track.

What next? I'd never been this far along the back road before and had to get out of the car to figure out how close to Foxton Ridge the route had brought me. Looking down from the high point, I could make out the creek winding through the valley and the old fishermen's shacks lining the banks. Farther away still was the small cluster of houses at the road junction, and up on the ridge facing me was the rock formation Phoenix had showed me called Angel Rock.

Close, but not close enough, I thought. To get to Hunter's place I had to walk along this new ridge and approach the ranch from the opposite direction of the route I usually took, a trek of maybe thirty minutes. Then again, I'd kept well out of sight and I knew I wouldn't be spotted by Bob Jonson and the guys from town before I reached Phoenix. Plus, I'd get there before dark and with luck my warning would be in time. I trudged west through the yuccas and sage, my feet crunching over the pale, gravelly soil, keeping my sights fixed on the landmark of Angel Rock. Soon my face was sweating in the heat, so I took off my jacket and tied it around my waist, glad for the breeze that blew off Amos Peak in the far distance.

Fifteen minutes passed. Angel Rock showed up black against the sinking red sun. I paused to wipe the back of my hand across my cheeks, hoping soon to catch sight of Phoenix and rehearsing the words I would say. "More trouble. The guys from town are definitely heading back here. Be ready."

The Beautiful Dead would be happy to see me. I would prove that I was worthy of their trust.

But as I walked on, the wind rose and slowed me down. It flapped at my shirt and tugged at the jacket slung around my hips. Dust blew in my face. I struggled on.

And then, as I reached Angel Rock, the wind turned into something else—fiercer and louder, bringing the rush of wings that beat down on me, forcing me to crouch in the deep shadow of the rock. "Stop!" I yelled. "Don't send me away. I'm here to help." The wings drowned out my voice, rising to a wave of sound, suffocating me, and battering me down to the ground.

I lay flat on my stomach, face to one side, watching the sun disappear and darkness fall like a blanket over the ridge. That was when I grew truly scared, but still I didn't turn and run.

Get through this, I told myself. *It's happened before—the wings, the force field driving you back. This time you know what you're dealing with.*

So I raised myself off the ground and began to stumble into the valley, with no hope now of finding another landmark or a point to head for, not in the pitch-black shadows of the mountain. So I slid and clutched at bushes, hit my shins against a fallen tree, gasped for breath, and kept on going.

Now my heart was beating fast and loud, the wind from the wings was tearing at me. I was breathless, filled with dread, almost defeated. *Why are you doing this to me?* I asked, crouching in the shelter of a tall rock.

I sensed a movement overhead and looked up into one of those skull faces with black holes where eyes should be, domed head and death-grin, swooping down, coming right at me, one and then another and another until my hands rose in panic and I was screaming just like the time before.

Strong hands lifted me up. I fought back, kicking and pulling free into the darkness, hearing footsteps follow me. They gained on me and I was caught again in the harsh grip.

"Stop!" I cried, turning, amazed to see I was being held by the woman who was the mother of the baby—one of Hunter's living dead. "Don't do this. You know me!" I cried.

Holding me by the arm, the woman dragged me back onto the ridge, her own hair torn back from her face, her features lost in shadow…the wings as loud as ever, the death faces, hovering.

I cried and struggled, fearful that I wouldn't get through to Phoenix and would suffer the ultimate punishment: I would be sent running with my mind wiped clear of everything that had happened. "Don't!" I pleaded. "I need to talk to Phoenix. He'll make you understand."

Hearing me speak his name, the woman suddenly let go of my arm and stepped back.

I slumped to the ground and when I looked up again, Phoenix was there, out of the blackness, gazing down at me.

"Darina." These arms were gentle as they helped me up. "I'm here now," he soothed. "Come with me. Take your time."

He made the wings stop and sent the zombie woman and the death heads away. My heart was already leaping for joy at seeing him again. "Hunter put us on high alert as soon as the sun began to set," he explained. "Eve was sent up here to protect the eastern boundary."

"The guys from town are coming back!" My own explanation was breathless, between low sobs that caught in my throat. I was relieved when I saw a soft glow of yellow light that meant we were close to the ranch house.

"Don't talk right now. Wait till we get inside." Phoenix guided me in the darkness over the old wooden doorstep into the ancient house. "Who's coming?" he asked as soon as he'd closed the door.

"Jonas's dad and a few others. They won't let it rest until they've found out what goes on up here."

He nodded. "Hunter said they'd be back. That's why he put us on alert. How many, do you know?"

"Not exactly." Catching my breath, I rolled up my jeans to see a bloody scratch on my shin where I'd fallen over the log. "Four or five maybe. Anyway, not as many as last time. So how come Eve used the wings against me?"

Phoenix made me sit down on the old rocking chair, then moved to the sink to fetch a basin of cold water and a clean hand towel. "We set it up so no one could get through. Eve heard a car in the distance and automatically put up the barrier. I'm sorry you got hurt."

"It's nothing." I winced as Phoenix dabbed the blood away. The moment he cleaned the skin, a pattern of tiny red spots reappeared, gathered, then slowly trickled to my ankle. I grimaced again then looked around the empty house.

"Where is everyone?"

"Out on the boundaries, keeping a lookout. Press hard on this towel, right here. It'll stop the bleeding."

"Why? Where are you going?"

"Nowhere. I need to speak with Jonas. Wait."

I watched Phoenix stand near the window, his eyelids semi-closed, a look of intense concentration on his face. "Hey, Jonas, it's Phoenix. How are you doing, dude?"

"Good," came the reply, as clear as if Jonas was in the room.

I looked round wildly, wondering what was going on.

"Where are you?"

"Up by the water tower. Where are you?"

"In the house."

"Who's with you? I can hear someone in the room."

"It's Darina. That's why I wanted to talk with you. She says your dad is heading back with a bunch of guys. Can you hear anything unusual up there?"

"Nope." Nevertheless, Jonas sounded worried. "How's Darina? Is she OK?"

"Yeah, pretty much. Eve didn't recognize her in the dark. She gave her a hard time. Listen, Jonas, you need to tell Hunter what's going to happen—about your dad and the others. They'll come up from Foxton, so get everyone in place ready."

"OK, leave it with me."

"And if you run up against your dad, don't get involved. Let the others do the work."

"Yeah, right." Jonas's voice began to fade as Phoenix relaxed and came away from the window. "Thanks, Phoenix. See you."

"See you, dude," he muttered.

"How did you do that?" I demanded, partly spooked but mostly amazed.

"Do what?"

"Talk to a guy half a mile away and make him sound like he was right here in the room?"

Phoenix smiled. "We hear everything, remember."

"Yeah, but how did you make me hear too?"

"I pumped up the volume for you, like we were on speakerphone. It would have been kind of rude to cut you out of the conversation."

"Just like that?" I relaxed and grinned. "You know how weird this all is for me, don't you?"

Phoenix's smile broadened then he drew me from the chair onto the floor where we sat cross-legged facing one another, close enough to lean forward and exchange a couple of sweet, gentle kisses. "Who told you that Bob and his bunch were going to try again?"

"He did," I explained. "I was at Charlie Fortune's

workshop, trying to find out more about Jonas's crash. Jonas's dad was there, telling Charlie the plan. That threw me off course, so I never had the chance to quiz Charlie about the repair he did on Jonas's Dyna. I headed out here instead. That could only happen after I'd gotten rid of your big brother. He did his best to slow me down, like always."

Phoenix tilted his head to one side and narrowed his eyes. "You talked with Brandon?"

"It's OK. He's being real nice, the same as he was after the funeral." And I told Phoenix about my reckless jump into the creek and how I had to be rescued by big bro. "Now he wants to find me a car."

Slowly Phoenix nodded.

"Are you OK with that?" I asked. "I guess it's Brandon's way of doing stuff for me, just like you asked."

"He told you that?" Phoenix seemed surprised, a little on edge.

"Yeah. He said you talked to him before you fell unconscious. You asked him to take care of me."

"I don't remember." He frowned then took my hands in his. "It's cool. You need someone, and Brandon doesn't take crap from anyone. Let him go ahead and find you a car."

"I don't care if he does or not." Gently I stroked the

insides of Phoenix's wrists then ran my hands up his arms, over the curves of his biceps so that my fingers rested on his shoulders. "Wouldn't it be cool to be living here in this house, just the two of us?"

"Yeah, with a fire in the grate and a lamp shining in the window. Corny, huh?" Phoenix closed his eyes. He leaned forward so that his cheek touched mine, tingling skin against skin.

"We'd take water from the creek and you'd chop logs while I baked bread, just like in Hunter's day." *Real* corny, but a twenty-first-century girl can dream herself back to frontier hominess.

"Hey, was Hunter married before—before he got shot?" I sat back a little, waiting for the answer.

Phoenix nodded. "That's *why* he got shot. He lived here with his wife, Marie. They spent six winters here, building the place up, farming cattle. Then a neighbor from Foxton made trouble. A guy called Peter Mentone. He came calling on Marie one day when Hunter was gone, with only one thing on his mind."

"Don't tell me." Images of Laura finding Dad with Karli Hamilton flashed through my memory—the shouting and screaming, the raw anger, the ugly secret sex, and the hurt.

"The way Hunter tells it, Marie wasn't interested in

Mentone and she was putting up a fight when Hunter came home unexpectedly. Hunter went crazy and tore at the guy with his bare hands. Mentone had a gun."

I shook my head and shuddered. "So now I have to feel sorry for Hunter." I sighed. "Who would've believed it?"

"Come here." Phoenix pulled me closer and the tingling turned into a shudder of desire. "What a dream that would be, you and me living together, twenty-four seven, forever. How does that sound?"

"Like heaven," I whispered. "Forever" seemed to echo around the room.

He kissed me and I melted into him, loving the closeness, my fingertips against his cool cheeks, his arms holding me.

"Answer a question for me." I didn't move, breathing the words against his lips. "Is it true what Jonas told me—the Beautiful Dead can't stay here forever?"

Phoenix held still. Too still. "Don't make me answer that, Darina."

"Jonas said a year." Phoenix was so close his eyes were blurred, the dark lashes curving downward as his eyelids fluttered shut again. *Better to know than not to know* said a masochistic voice inside my head. "Is it true?"

"Twelve whole months," he murmured. "I'm with you for a long, long time."

Tears spilled down my cheeks. "But it's not long enough," I whispered. "It's not forever."

6

Hunter must have still been expecting the bikers to arrive by the usual route. He'd posted most of his lookouts on the water tower ridge, with only Eve and Phoenix out on the wilderness to the east.

That meant Eve was alone up by Angel Rock when Bob Jonson and the others took her by surprise.

Phoenix heard the engines and called Summer and Hunter to come down from Foxton Ridge and head for Angel Rock instead. "The guys came across country," he explained, pacing the room. "Eve's holding back some of them, but not all."

Now even I could hear the bikes. And I could see shafts of bright light from their headlights raking across the hillsides.

"Will you stay here with me?" I asked Phoenix.

He nodded. "We can't risk anyone finding you. Turn out the kitchen lights and come upstairs."

We crept up into the one and only bedroom that Hunter had shared with his wife, Marie. We closed the drapes, held hands, leaned against the wall, and kept out of sight.

Outside, the ridge was crisscrossed by beams of light. I pictured the Beautiful Dead beating back the approach of the bikers, driving them crazy with the sound of wings and the sight of death heads, sending them back the way they'd come.

"We're doing good," Phoenix reported, listening to messages I couldn't hear. "Hunter and Summer are up there with Eve. Two of the guys have already turned around."

I nodded. It was weird how calm I felt around Phoenix, as if he were my magic, impenetrable shield.

"But they're having trouble with one guy," Phoenix said, listening closely. "They don't know who it is. It's dark and he's wearing a helmet. He's on a bike they haven't seen before."

I heard the whine of an engine speeding along the ridge. Then the rider turned at the water tower and pointed his bike down into the valley, his headlight juddering over the rough ground as he sped nearer.

"He got past Eve," Phoenix muttered, letting go of my hand and peering between the drapes.

The bike was close to the house, swerving recklessly around boulders, near enough to make out its dark rider and the glint of his visor.

"Stay down!" Phoenix ordered. "Don't move!"

I watched him sprint across the room and heard him run

downstairs two at a time. Then I crept to the window and peered down, hearing Phoenix burst through the door just as the rider braked and let his bike drop to the ground. I saw him wrench off his helmet in the moonlight. It was Jonas's dad.

Phoenix stayed well in the shadow of the house, watching warily, waiting for Bob Jonson to make his next move.

Jonson flung his helmet to one side. He knew there was someone in the shadows of the porch but he couldn't see who it was, so he stood wide-legged like a wary gunslinger.

"Come out of there," he ordered. "Or I come in. You choose."

I held my breath, wondering what Phoenix's next move would be. Wondering too what kind of desperation had driven Bob Jonson to ignore the supernatural warnings up by Angel Rock and do what none of his biker friends had had the guts to do.

"OK, I'm coming for you," he warned, and took a deliberate step toward the shadows.

When Phoenix stepped out I knew it was because he wanted to protect me. No way would he let Jonson find me in the house. He stood in the moonlight face-to-face.

For a few seconds nothing happened. Bob Jonson's brain took awhile to compute what he was seeing. A young guy with dark hair, his face pale in the moonlight, his expression blank. Then Jonson's suspicious, angry face changed. The frown deepened, his mouth went slack as he took a sharp breath and muttered one word—"Phoenix."

Phoenix blinked. He made the wings beat louder and stronger, caused the dust in the yard to whirl up, and made the intruder put his hand to his eyes.

Back off, Bob. Get the hell out! I warned silently from the bedroom window.

"They said you died," Jonson said in a low, growling voice. "They held your funeral and all."

Still Phoenix said nothing. He was using all his power to turn Jonson away, just as Eve had done before him. But I knew Bob Jonson didn't care if he lived or died. He was beyond scaring. He was a shell, left only with his grief.

"What the hell's going on?" he muttered, closing the gap between him and Phoenix. "If you're alive, who knows, maybe my boy Jonas is too."

Speak to him, Phoenix. Throw him off the scent, I thought, pulling back the drape to get a clearer view.

Jonson caught the movement out of the corner of his eye. He glanced up and saw my face, recognized me right away. "Darina, you get down here!" he yelled.

My stomach lurched as I ducked out of sight. I heard another shout—Jonson calling my name again then scuffling with Phoenix.

"Back off, I've got a gun," he warned. Then silence.

I froze and listened to footsteps on the wooden porch and the thud of what sounded like Jonson thrusting Phoenix aside.

That was it. I broke cover and darted downstairs in time to find Phoenix wrestling Jonson back from the door and Jonson waving a small handgun in his face.

"I swear I'll use it," he threatened us both.

"Get back, Darina!" Phoenix flung himself at Jonson and tried to grapple the gun away from him. The rocking chair went crashing against the old stove as the two guys fell headlong on the floor.

Jonson fired one shot. A small cracking sound, not a *boom-boom* like I'd imagined. So what did I do? My mind went blank and I went crazy. I ran at the guy with the gun to save my boyfriend, who was already dead. Yeah. It made perfect sense.

There was a second shot before Phoenix finally managed to grab the gun and hand it to me, leaving him free to keep Jonson pinned down. My hands trembled at the feel of cold steel, at the weight of it, heavier than I'd thought…but still I pointed the barrel of the gun right at Jonson's head.

He looked up at me, totally calm, waiting for me to shoot.

"Get up, but don't make another move," Phoenix told him, pulling him onto his feet by the front of his sheepskin jacket.

I kept my trembling aim. What was I doing? I'd never held a gun before in my life.

"Don't look at Darina, look at me," Phoenix told him quietly. "I said, ignore Darina!"

Jonson's eyes had flicked in my direction, judging whether or not I would pull the trigger.

"This is what will happen," Phoenix went on, keeping hold of Jonson and pushing him back toward the kitchen door. Outside, the dust still whirled and millions of wings flapped up a storm. "You're going to pick up your bike and start the engine. You're going to ride right out of here."

"I'm not leaving," Jonson argued. "I need answers. You tell me what happened. Where's my boy?"

"You're going to ride right out of here without looking back," Phoenix repeated slowly. "I'm going to do something now that won't feel good, Bob. It'll seem like someone knocked you hard on the head."

"You take your hands off me!" Jonson started to fight back, even though I was still aiming the gun.

One squeeze of the trigger…

Trust me, Darina, Phoenix's voice said, though he didn't open his mouth and there was no sound.

"I'm going to do it now," Phoenix told Jonson. "I'm going to wipe what happened here from your memory—totally zap it. Like I said, you'll have a sore head, but you won't recall a thing."

Jonson grew frantic and struggled again. "You're talking crazy. This whole thing is crazy!"

Phoenix was stronger by far. He forced Jonson out into the open, down into the dirt and the weeds, right beside the rusting truck.

Jonson was half up again, crouching, ready to throw himself forward at Phoenix, when Phoenix concentrated—*zap!* The hypnotic attack on Jonson's memory threw him back down and sprawling in the dirt, writhing in pain, and rolling away from his attacker, who hadn't even raised a finger. Again—*zap!* And the wings beat louder, shrouding the bike, the truck, and us in thick white dust.

After Bob Jonson put on his helmet and rode away, Phoenix gently unclasped my fingers from the gun. He slid it into his pocket and pulled me into his arms. Then we stood in the moonlight waiting for everything to get back to normal. Or close enough.

"Hunter will be here soon," he murmured. "Jonas's dad was the last to leave. The rest already rode out."

"Oh God, Phoenix, what's happening to me?" I couldn't believe I'd actually pointed the gun and thought about pulling the trigger.

"You panicked when you heard he was armed," he replied.

"I was stupid to let him see me," I argued. "I made things worse." Plus, I'd contemplated shooting a guy. Not a stranger: someone I knew, someone who was suffering.

"Don't beat yourself up." Phoenix looked at me earnestly, doing his best to convince me. "It worked out. Jonson will get back to town and he won't remember a single thing that happened from the time he rode down from the ridge to the point where he got back onto the Ellerton road."

"You're certain?" I was still shaking, even though his arms were around me.

"Totally." He stepped back and looked deep into my eyes. "Here comes Hunter," he warned without turning around.

I stood on tiptoe to peer over his shoulder. Sure enough, Hunter, Jonas, Summer, Arizona, and Eve were walking through the meadow at the back of the barn, the silvery grass brushing their legs as they came slowly toward us. They looked exhausted.

"Are we all safe?" Phoenix asked, releasing me and standing by my side.

Hunter nodded. "I left Donna in charge of the baby up in the hayloft. Iceman is on his way down from Twelve O'clock Rock." As he finished talking he leaned wearily against the truck.

"How many did we zap?" Arizona asked, sitting on the porch step.

"Only one—Jonas's dad." Hunter sighed, head back and eyes closed. "Thanks to Darina and the fact that she can't follow orders."

"I did warn you what she was like," Arizona reminded him. "Hey, Phoenix, did you tell your girlfriend that every time we have to wipe someone's memory it weakens the whole group? No, I guess you didn't."

"What does she mean?" I asked Phoenix.

His gaze flickered. "It takes a whole lot of energy for us to control a person's mind that way, so we're less strong, our hearing isn't so good, stuff like that."

"I didn't realize," I whispered.

Summer came forward and gave me the gift of one of her special smiles. "Don't worry, Darina. Our powers get back to normal once we've rested."

"Hey, Iceman, how was it up at Twelve O'clock Rock?" Eve asked the newcomer, who had just crossed the creek and was approaching the group.

He was the short, wiry guy, with fair hair cropped close to his head. I recognized him as the one I'd previously seen with Eve, Donna, and the baby.

"Nothing happening," he reported. "Jonas, you OK?"

"Cool," Jonas nodded.

"I'm sorry about your dad, man. I hope he doesn't come back for a third round of punishment."

"Yeah, he's going to feel like he did twelve rounds with a professional heavyweight," Arizona said, studying me for my reaction.

I couldn't find any point to make in my own defense so I hung my head and stayed quiet.

"Hey, why so hard on Darina?" Summer had stayed by my side and spoke up for me now. "She was the one who came to warn us, remember?"

"And the one who didn't get anywhere with Zoey Bishop yet." Hunter spoke up, and of course he was against me, not for me. "We don't need you driving out here and showing yourself to our enemies. It's not helpful."

In that respect, he was right. "I'm sorry," I told him.

"Don't be sorry. Be useful. Jonas, walk Darina to her car. She parked out beyond Angel Rock. Summer, Arizona, and Eve, get some rest. Phoenix too."

I frowned and made as if to ask Phoenix to come with me, feeling my heart jolt and my stomach tighten at the prospect of leaving him again.

"Go with Jonas," he told me softly. And he kissed me long and hard on the lips, even though Hunter was giving us his cold stare.

So that's what I did—I kissed him back and walked away

under the moon and stars, across rough ground with Jonas
at my side.

We didn't speak for a long time.

"I'm sorry," I told Jonas at last. "I didn't do it deliberately—
let your dad see me, I mean. He had a gun. I was scared."

"It's cool." Paler than ever in the bright moonlight, Jonas's
eyes seemed more hooded, the pupils enormous in his pale
blue irises. "It would've happened anyway. My dad doesn't
care anymore. I keep expecting him to ride his bike straight
into a rock—to end it all."

"To be with you?"

"Yeah. That's why he bought the Dyna—to be the same
as me, to bring him closer."

"You're guessing," I argued. "You don't know for sure."

"I've seen the way he rides and the look on his face.
It's death."

I sighed, stopping for breath as we reached the summit of a
smooth domed rock. "Doesn't your dad have anyone else?"

"Only Mom. Since my crash the doctor's been giving her
medication. Right now she's with her sister in Chicago,
taking a break from Dad and everything."

I didn't need to ask what Jonas meant by "everything."
Given the fact that the inquest had just delivered its verdict,
it wasn't difficult to see why his mom had moved out for a
while. "I wish I could do more," I muttered.

We struck out along a ridge that would bring us to my car, each lost in our own thoughts until Jonas went off on a new track. "Hunter gives you a hard time."

"He scares me," I admitted.

"Summer has a theory about it." Jonas walked with his hands in his pockets, kicking small stones against rocks as he walked. "Do you want to know?"

"You people talk about me?" I was surprised.

"Sure, we do. You're our only interesting topic of conversation."

"Apart from the god-awful things that happened to you all in the last twelve months."

"They're always the same. They don't change. Except if *you* make them change for us, Darina. We depend on you."

"Me?" Suddenly it hit me that what I had to do was huge—first help Jonas, then move on to Arizona, and so on down the line. It was too much. "So what's Summer's theory?" I asked, taking a jump sideways away from the high-octane responsibility.

"Summer believes Hunter is hard on you for a reason," Jonas said.

"More than just because I'm an idiot who keeps on getting stuff wrong?"

"You're not an idiot. Listen. Summer once saw an old picture that Hunter keeps in his pocket. It fell out when he took his shirt off to swim in the creek—a picture of a woman."

"His wife, Marie?" I guessed.

"Yeah. You know the story? Well, Summer took a peek at the photograph. It was kind of brown and faded, but she could make out that Marie looked a lot like you—the same dark hair, the same eyes. Even the smile."

"Wow." I thought for a while. "I remind him of her. So why is he mean to me? Oh, I get it—it's a painful memory and it's turned him against me."

"Even though it's no way your fault," Jonas agreed. "Which proves something about Hunter."

"What exactly?" I asked urgently. Jonas and I were reaching the end of our walk. I could see my car windshield gleaming in the moonlight, about a quarter of a mile ahead.

"That he does still have feelings breaking through, even after all these years. That he's not made of ice, although he wants everyone to believe he is."

Hunter, the unfeeling overlord of the Beautiful Dead, the ruthless avenger. Or Hunter, who died to save Marie, the man who loved his wife more than his life.

Take your pick.

On Sundays Jim is usually home. It's no big deal. He's in the house and I try to ignore him.

But that Sunday, after I'd told Jonas good-bye and promised him that I'd try to visit Zoey again as soon as I could, it turned out I couldn't keep out of Jim's sight line for more than five minutes at a time. Apparently, my grieving time was up in his book.

First it was, "Darina, take the trash out for your mom," then, "Have you cleaned your room?" and "How are you going to pay to get your fender fixed?" Yackety-yak, on and on with the banal, boring stuff, like he really wanted to nail me. But after four years of it, I'm pretty well immune.

"Darina, why can't you try being nice, just once?" Laura asked when Jim drove to the store to buy milk and a newspaper.

"Why can't *he* try being nice?" I snapped back. "He knows what I've been through."

Laura was doing Sunday chores with the TV switched on in the kitchen and the dishwasher swirling and swishing in the background. Not looking her best, I'd say, in one of Jim's gray-white sweatshirts and a pair of faded jogging pants, with her hair scraped back and her face looking saggy.

That's the bitch in me coming through, and maybe Laura picked it up in the way I was staring at her, because all of a sudden she grabbed a cloth and began to rub hard at invisible specks of dirt on the side of the refrigerator. "I can't take this anymore," she muttered. "You and Jim need to get along, or else I'm out of here." The manic cleaning meant she was serious. "I mean it. I've had enough of the bad atmosphere between you two. Darina, I need you to acknowledge that Jim is the man I love and *chose* to live with. Also, that, even though you're grieving for Phoenix, it still doesn't make you the most important person in the world."

"I'm not even the most important person in this room," I argued. "Hey, I come way down the list: after Jim, somewhere around cleaning the house, and watching your favorite TV program."

Laura stopped the polishing routine and stood with her back to me. "You're so young," she murmured, sighing as she stared out of the window.

Where did that come from? Her sideswipe made me step back.

Laura turned toward me with tears in her eyes. "You still think life is simple, don't you, Darina? Either black or white, right or wrong."

I frowned, then nodded. "So I have opinions. So what?"

Laura brushed the tears away and picked up her cloth again. "I guess I remember being that way when I was your age."

"But not anymore?"

"No. Right now things are way more complicated than I

ever dreamed. Most days I'm walking a tightrope—should I do this, say that, jump this way, or that? Every second of every day I'm just trying to keep my balance."

"Because of Jim?" I asked carefully. "Or because of me?"

"Because of both of you. And you know what I do, Darina? I clean the house and I go to work in the clothes store, because that way I don't *have* to think."

I shook my head slowly, meaning that was no way to live. But we'd run out of time because Jim's car door slammed and he came into the house with the news that the whole of Ellerton was buzzing again with rumors about Foxton Ridge, and that Laura needed to ground me for at least a week for wrecking my car…and how he didn't want any more trouble until the wild ghost stories had had time to die down and the town could get back to normal.

No way is he going to ground me.

I got this mantra going inside my head and snuck out of the house late on Sunday afternoon, the second Jim's back was turned. Or rather, the second he fell asleep in front of the television.

I bought gas at the station where Phoenix had died then drove by Charlie Fortune's place, expecting it to be closed Sundays, and sure enough the security gate was locked in front of the window, the gleaming Harleys stored safely behind.

This didn't put me off tracking down Charlie because I knew where he lived—in a block of apartments overlooking the mall. Also, I'd promised Jonas I'd work on solving his crash situation before his time on the far side was up—nine days from now.

"I'll talk to Charlie tomorrow," I'd promised in the moonlight, up near the tree line where the pines gave way to sage scrub and bare rock. "He just might let slip a tiny fact about the work he did to fix your bike."

Jonas had concentrated all his hopes in the intense stare he gave me before he said good-bye. "Try everything," he whispered. "But don't be hard on Zoey next time you see her."

I'd nodded and kissed him on the cheek. My heart was wrung out and aching for him. I'd touched the belt buckle in my pocket then driven off.

So, braving the garbage bins and dirty elevator at the entrance to Charlie's building was no big deal, nor was the nasty graffiti or a big guy sitting in a rickety chair, staring me up and down as I walked along the balcony to Charlie's apartment and knocked at the door.

"What's up?" the guy in the chair wanted to know.

"I came to see Charlie." I gave the insultingly obvious reply.

"Not home. Only Matt."

I wished I could take back the knock on the door. I didn't

move away in time to avoid Matt, who opened it, saw it was me, and was about to slam it in my face, then changed his mind.

"Darina, good to see you. You're looking good," he said, his voice loaded with insult that contradicted the words he spoke.

I didn't blink or give him the satisfaction of a response.

"Kind of pale and tragic. It suits you," he added.

This made me want to get back at him. "I thought you were out at Foxton with Christian. Oh no, I remember now—your big brother reeled you back in."

He bristled. "Is that what you heard?"

"Yeah. You boys are scared of ghosts."

"But not you, huh?" Matt suddenly came toward me, edging into my personal space, forcing me back against the balcony railing. There was a four-story drop to ground level. "From what Logan says, you're acting weird, Darina. You spend a lot of time up there, don't you?"

"Where I spend my time is none of Logan's business," I muttered, trying to duck underneath Matt's arm.

"But Logan would like it to be." Matt sneered, trapping me again. "I've seen the way he stares at you lately. But I told him, Darina looks hot but underneath she's cold as ice. I should know."

This did it for me. I squared up to Matt Fortune and gave

it to him straight. "Hard as it is for you to believe, not every girl is ready to fall at your feet. As a matter of fact, no single girl I know is taken in by the cheesy smile and the leather jacket, not after what you did to Zoey."

Matt's eyelids flickered. His nose was only inches from my own. "Why? What did I do to Zoey?"

I pushed against his chest. "OK, Matt, that's exactly what I mean. You ditch her in front of everyone—at a party, for God's sake. And you make a move on her best friend—also in public. Yet you don't see it as a problem."

"Oh, that," he snorted. "Zoey's a drama queen."

"And I'm the Ice Maiden." I pushed hard and got away at last. "Have it your way, Matt. Just tell Charlie I want to talk with him, OK?"

He laughed. "You want to buy a Harley?"

"Maybe," I retorted, walking past the guy at his door.

"Charlie's way too old for you, Darina!" Matt yelled after me. "And way out of your league!"

"Or maybe not," the neighbor muttered with a wink.

I ran down the stairs feeling dirty, angry, and all of three inches tall.

I was home that evening, but my head was all over the place. I was up at Foxton Ridge hearing the barn door banging all over again and over at Zoey's house. I was remembering happy times with Summer and the unspoken pressure Logan had been putting me under lately.

But most of all I was with Phoenix: hearing his voice, feeling his arms around me, drinking in how it made me tingle and shudder.

I paced inside my room, wearing out the rug.

Phoenix: with a lock of dark hair falling over his forehead; his eyes fringed with heavy lashes; his full lips and wonderful pale skin; the small angel wings tattooed on his perfect body between his shoulder blades…and restless, unable to find peace, like me.

"I love you," I whispered, looking out of the window toward the dark mountains, seeing the neon crucifix way in the distance on the hill.

Laura knocked on the door and came in. She'd scrubbed up for the evening—makeup and hair, white shirt with a frill down the front, black pants. "I just took a call from Brandon Rohr. Didn't you hear the phone ring?" I shook my head. "What did he want?" I asked.

"He said to tell you he'd found you a car."

"Jeez." I sighed.

"How come, Darina?"

"Don't ask me."

"Did he promise Phoenix he'd take care of you?"

I nodded. "I guess."

"But where did he find the car? It's not stolen, is it?"

I turned my stare on her and froze her out. "Oh yeah, definitely stolen. Like, he'd give his dead brother's girlfriend a car that could get her thrown in jail."

"I'll ask Jim to talk to him," Laura stated, closing my door as my cell phone began to ring.

It was Mrs. Bishop calling from their house. "Darina, I know it's late but can you come visit Zoey?"

"Now?" I asked.

"As soon as you can. I wouldn't ask, but it's important."

"Mrs. Bishop, what's wrong?" Her voice was breaking up.

"Bob Jonson was here earlier, putting pressure on Zoey. He was sure Zoey could remember the crash, that she was faking her memory loss. I think he's gone a little crazy. In the end Russell told him to leave."

"That sounds bad," I said. I pictured Jonas's dad hammering on the Bishops' door, his head still sore and his memory zapped.

"My husband threw him out. Zoey was beginning to relive some of the details, but all mixed up and not making any sense."

"Oh, but that could be good," I gasped. It didn't have to be me who kick-started Zoey's memory—I would be fine with whatever it took.

Her mom didn't agree. "We don't want her to relive the

trauma without supervision. We called Kim Reiss to see if she could come round, but it's Sunday so she's out of town. That's when Zoey asked for you."

By this time I'd left my room and was practically out of the front door, reaching for my car keys on the hook.

"Where are you going?" Jim called, clearly ready to give me a fight.

"*Mom,* Zoey needs me," I replied over my shoulder, deliberately ignoring him. "I'll be there," I told Mrs. Bishop over the phone. "Give me ten minutes."

"Hurry," she said. "I'm scared. Zoey's falling apart in front of our eyes."

7

see him!" Zoey clutched my hand as I stood beside her wheelchair and pointed across the room. "Jonas is right here, in this room!"

I alone knew it wasn't as crazy as it sounded. But when I checked, the room was empty. "I hear you," I told her. "Zoey, don't be scared."

It was as if she hadn't heard me. "Tell them to go away," she pleaded.

"Who?" Mr. and Mrs. Bishop had already left, after Zoey had yelled at them to go almost the moment I'd arrived.

"Mom and Dad. They're smothering me." She seemed to fight the air, her eyes unfocused, cold sweat standing out on her brow.

"OK, I've told them to go. They left us alone." I tried to calm her.

"I can't breathe. I can't move. Jonas, what happened?"

"Hush," I whispered. I pulled up a chair beside her and sat facing her in the brightly lit room—too brightly lit for my taste. With the bottles of pills by the night table and the bed neatly made, it felt like a hospital room. But maybe that was deliberate. Who could blame her parents for freaking out? I could see she had taken herself to another place and was hyperventilating. "Take deep breaths."

"He's gone!" she wailed, holding on to me all the harder. "He was right here, trying to tell me something. He spoke, but I didn't hear the words."

I fought to stay calm. "I'm here. It's me, Darina. Try to breathe."

Slowly she stopped panting and began to draw air deeper into her lungs. "I want Jonas to come back," she sobbed.

I felt her pain like it was my own. Zoey and Jonas. Me and Phoenix. We were equal. Except she'd had no contact, no knowledge of the Beautiful Dead.

"What do you want to tell him?" I murmured.

"I love him. I'll always love him." Her face, distorted with grief and wet with tears, tugged at my heart.

I knelt and put my arms around her shoulders. "What else?"

"I want him to come back."

My heart stopped. One sentence from me and I could make it happen for her.

Let me take you to Foxton Ridge to see Jonas. But it would destroy them all.

Instead, I took her hand in my own. "I know what you're going through," I whispered.

"I knew you would. But, Darina, do you ever talk about it?"

"No."

"Not even to your mom?"

"No way."

"Me neither. To Logan maybe?"

"No. Not to anyone."

"I have visions," Zoey confessed. "Sometimes I see Jonas riding his bike in the blinding sun. I'm calling his name but he's riding away from me along a narrow, winding road, and the metal on his bike is flashing and gleaming. Other times I'm riding on the back and the wind is in my hair and my arms are around his waist. It ends in a terrible noise and blackness."

"I know," I murmured. I couldn't trust myself to say any more.

"And then afterward I hear him. He's leaning over me and his voice is a long way off, telling me he's sorry. Just that—over and over. And I try to say it's not his fault, but the words won't come off my tongue. They just roll around my mouth like it's full of pebbles, and he's gone before I can say them, and all I can hear is a kind of wind sighing through the darkness—more like wings beating, hundreds of them, maybe thousands— and then nothing. Jonas has gone and I'm saying, 'It's not your fault,' and I lose the vision and then I'm alone and I can't bear it—not another day, not another hour or minute."

"You have to bear it," I told her in a shaky voice. "For Jonas's sake." *And because I need you to get your memory back.* Not just in flashes, or visions, as she called them, but coolly, and in the right order, able to go through the fatal moments with a clear head.

"I feel so lonely," Zoey repeated.

"You're not alone. Jonas may be gone, but you have me." I crouched down in front of her wheelchair so that she had to look me in the eye. "You know you can trust me."

Some old doubt in her messed-up head made Zoey suddenly draw back.

"How can I be sure?"

"Because we've been friends forever."

"Except for what happened with Matt," she said, pushing away from me. "You humiliated me."

"I already told you, that was all Matt. Why won't you believe me?"

"The way he told it, you did all the chasing—before Hannah's party and afterward."

"He's lying." I didn't want to rake over old dirt, but I knew Zoey was still angry and wouldn't let this go until I told her what she wanted to hear, or she accepted my version of what really happened. "He probably wanted to get back with you, so he decided to rewrite history."

Zoey nodded. "He did try to get back, it's true. He came on to me in school the next day."

"Matt isn't a good guy. He thinks he's irresistible, plus he's a sore loser. Listen, forget about Matt and talk to me about Jonas. What are you trying to tell him in your flashback, the part where he says sorry? It's straight after the crash, isn't it?"

Slowly Zoey nodded. "That's how come I can't speak. I'm lying in the road and I can hardly breathe. I only see his face."

"I know, it happens so fast. It's a hot day. One moment you're riding in the sun, the next it's over. Something happened and you're trying to figure it out."

She nodded again, staring into space with a haunted look. "It wasn't Jonas's fault. That's what I'm saying. I'm telling him there was something else…"

"A car coming toward you on the wrong side of the road? A deer jumping out at you?" I suggested whatever popped into my head—and instantly regretted it, realizing none of it would help.

"Neither of those things." Zoey was trying hard to concentrate, to literally bring it all back together and make it make sense. I was holding my breath and gripping one of the wheels of her chair hard. "I'm lying on the road and Jonas is kind of hovering over me. It feels like he's floating."

"Go back further. Before that, what happened?"

"Jonas crashed the bike," she murmured. "Something went wrong."

"What happened?" I begged. "Was it the bike? Did a tire blow? Was it the brakes?"

"No." Zoey blinked then seemed to give up. Her body sagged forward. "I don't know. I can't remember."

"You're doing great," I told her, stroking her hair and noticing that Mrs. Bishop had quietly opened the door. "Next time we talk, you'll remember more."

"Hey, honey," Zoey's mom said. "You're exhausted. It's time for Darina to leave."

Zoey didn't object. Instead she drew a deep sigh and shook her head. "Sorry," she murmured.

I squeezed her hand and tried to smile. "No problem. Get some sleep. I'll drop by again tomorrow."

So I left her with her mom and walked straight into big, bad Daddy Bear waiting for me at the front door.

"Don't count on coming back anytime soon," Mr. Bishop warned. "I'm the guy who monitors my daughter's visitors, and I'm not impressed by your influence over Zoey, Darina."

"Your wife called and asked me to come." What else could I say? I shrugged and tried to walk out of the door.

"I heard most of what went on in there," he said, still standing in my way in his crisp red checked shirt and navy blue chinos. "And I've told you already, I don't like the way you're trying to drag her back into traumas she can't deal with."

I'd faced enough obstacles for one day and Russell Bishop was one too many. "You're the ones who baby her and protect her from the reality of what happened."

Small muscles in his neck twitched and he jerked his head forward. "My daughter is seventeen years old and she can't walk," he hissed. "This family faces the reality of what happened to her every day of our lives!"

Ouch. I blinked then nodded. "Sorry. But Mrs. Bishop did call me. Zoey needed to talk."

"Zoey is too injured to know what she needs," Mr. Bishop insisted, opening the door and showing me out. "But I'm her dad, and I make the decisions on her behalf. So I'm telling you, Darina, we only let you into the house tonight because Zoey was out of control and we had no way of getting the experts in here. We gave into her demands, but don't expect it to happen again."

"Even if your wife calls me?" Mr. Bishop stared straight through me. "Good-bye, Darina," he said as he closed the door.

The next day I woke up early and there was a shiny red convertible sitting in the drive.

"It's yours," Laura told me, dangling the keys from her little finger. "Brandon Rohr dropped it off earlier."

"So now I believe in Santa Claus," Jim mumbled on his way out of the house.

"He drove your old car away," Laura said. It was obvious that she didn't know how to judge Brandon's motives. "You and Brandon—you're not…dating?"

"Please!" I snorted, taking the keys from her. "He was doing me a favor Phoenix asked him to do."

"Is it on loan, or do you get to keep it?" She came to the door and watched me start the engine—no clunking or coughing, just a smooth purr.

"I have no idea." I really didn't. "Anyhow, I'm taking it on a test drive through Centennial."

"So ask Brandon next time you see him. And tell him I need to check the paperwork!"

I waved and backed onto the street, then turned at the junction to head toward Foxton with nothing in my head except testing my new red car. Well, hardly anything. I thought about Phoenix, of course. If it weren't for him, Brandon wouldn't have made the gesture.

Sweet, I thought, halfway to becoming a car nut before

I'd even been driving it for five minutes. Smooth suspension, great acceleration, and the cutest set of dials in front of me, with a neat, beige leather steering wheel to top it off. Who cared if the paperwork didn't check out?

I was so jazzed I almost didn't see Phoenix and Jonas at first.

They were standing by the side of the road where it splits and the narrow track takes off the back way toward Angel Rock—two figures under a tree, looking like two regular guys, getting ready to hitch a ride.

I stopped, leaned over, and opened the passenger door.

Phoenix crouched down, determined not to be impressed by my fancy new mode of transport.

"Hey, you."

Please just keep standing there with the sun making a halo around your head and let me drink in every inch of you.

"Hey. Get in, you two, and let's take a ride," was what I actually said.

He shook his head. "Turn the car off the road. We need to talk."

"OK." Feeling deflated, I drove onto the track then got out of the car. My face was flushed with embarrassment. "Sorry, I'm an airhead."

Phoenix's face broke into a smile. "You were having fun. I'm sorry we spoiled it. Did my brother give you the car?"

I nodded. "It was super-nice of him. Although I know I really have you to thank. What do we need to talk about?" I asked, locking onto Jonas's grim expression and joining him under the tree. "You know I went to see Zoey?"

"Late last night," he nodded. "How is she?"

I paused. "She's still having a tough time. Her folks called me over because she was in meltdown. It's OK, Jonas, I wasn't mean to her."

A truck hurtled down the highway toward Ellerton, quickly followed by a car, so Phoenix drew us around the far side of the tree. "And you, Darina—did Zoey's mood drag you down?"

"No, I'm good, thanks. I told her I knew how she felt, lonely and lost, and she said how much she still loves you, Jonas. It helped to share. And she's remembering more about the crash, so that's cool."

Phoenix put his arm around my shoulder then twisted his finger through the end of my hair. "Did she give you anything new?"

"Stuff about lying in the road after it happened and finding she couldn't move. She said you were there, Jonas, still alive and saying sorry."

Phoenix held me tighter. "Jonas died at the moment of impact," he reminded me. "It was his spirit Zoey saw and heard."

I nodded, remembering the sound of beating wings that she'd spoken about. I ought to have realized sooner.

"Anything else?" Jonas asked.

I shook my head. "Zoey's mom and dad must have been listening at the door. Mrs. Bishop broke in before I could push Zoey any farther down memory lane. She was right, Zoey was exhausted by what she'd already remembered. So, there was nothing solid she could tell me about the moments before the crash."

"And then what?" Phoenix asked, reading my face and guessing there was something I still hadn't told them.

"Mr. Bishop…" I began my answer then stopped with a shrug.

"He barred you from the house?" Phoenix guessed.

"Yeah. He doesn't like me, or anyone from my side of the tracks as a matter of fact."

"That's because your side of the tracks is where he started out," Jonas told me. "Twenty years ago the guy didn't have a cent. Then, the way Zoey tells it, he got lucky and married money."

Which explained a lot, I guess. "You know your dad also went to the Bishops' house?"

My news surprised even Jonas and Phoenix. "We didn't track him after he left us," Phoenix said. "What did he want?"

"He yelled and swapped insults. I don't know exactly,

except that it made things worse. Now Mr. Bishop wants to shut out the whole world."

"And we don't get any more answers," Jonas sighed.

"Right. Not unless I bump into Zoey again this Thursday at Kim Reiss's clinic." I saw one small glimmer of light in Jonas's eyes. "I'll make sure to do that," I promised him. "I'll go early and make time for us to talk one-on-one."

Jonas nodded then glanced down the highway. "Car coming," he reported, before it drove into sight.

"It's Logan!" At a glance I knew who it was in the clean white Honda. "What's he doing out this way?"

"Following you," Phoenix guessed again—accurately as it turned out.

"Go!" I told him and Jonas. "I'll handle this."

When I said, "Go!" I meant hide behind the tree or a rock. But no—Phoenix and Jonas disappeared. I mean, they dematerialized right there in front of my eyes. One moment they were solid, then they were wavy at the edges and see-through, then they weren't there at all.

"Hey, come back!" I cried as Logan signaled and pulled off the road.

"Who were you talking to?" he asked as he jumped out of his car.

"Logan, what are you doing here?" I demanded, ignoring the question.

"Checking up on you." He was totally open, as if he were doing me a favor.

I glared at him. "How did you know where I was?"

"I called at your house. Your mom told me about your new car and said you took it on a test drive before school. I promised I'd make sure you got to where you were meant to be—safe behind a desk."

"I'm not a kid. You have to quit following me," I told him angrily. Phoenix and Jonas's latest trick had thrown me way off balance, and I had the feeling they were still around, listening in on my conversation with Logan. "I'm starting to feel like you're a creepy stalker guy."

Logan's features wrinkled into a frown. "How can you say that?"

"Because, you're always there." I stepped by him to get into my car, but he caught hold of me.

"Darina, I know you don't want to hear this, but I'm still worried about the way you're acting. So is your mom. We all are."

"I've told you before, there's no need. Let go of my arm, Logan, you're hurting me."

"And I care about you," he went on in a robotic voice. This was a speech that he'd rehearsed over and over, I could tell. "I care a lot about you, Darina. I want us to be..." He didn't finish.

"Let me go," I pleaded after a split second of jaw-dropping astonishment. This time he was really going to kiss me unless I acted fast. "Logan, how can we be whatever it is you want us to be? I've known you forever."

"So?" He leaned in.

"We're like brother and sister!" This was crazy. Logan Lavelle had ideas of true romance and my beautiful Phoenix was hanging around invisibly watching it happen. I snatched at the closest straw. "Anyway, Logan, your timing is lousy. I'm still not over Phoenix."

Logan heard the name and stopped. He seemed equally stunned. "You mean, I'm competing with a dead guy?"

"You'd better believe it. Did you really think I could just forget him? Is that the kind of person you think I am?" I didn't get Logan anymore. Surely he knew how it felt to lose someone you loved.

"But he's gone, Darina. Phoenix is not coming back."

"Leave me alone," I whispered as I pulled away.

A part of Logan's brain seemed to register some of what was going on, but not all. He looked sorry for me, paused, then spoke again. "OK, Darina, I get it. It's too soon."

"*Much* too soon," I said, calmer now and able to get into the car.

"So I'll wait until you're over him," he promised, as if time was the biggest gift he could give me. "I'll wait for as long as it takes."

There was a time, before Phoenix, when Logan and I could practically read each other's thoughts. We went everywhere as a pair, liked the same things, spoke the same language. Truth be told: I missed that simple, sunshine togetherness of kids' sharing. But even if Phoenix had never happened, there was no way I could be Logan's girlfriend.

That night after school, I had time to try and figure it out. I found my scrapbook under a pile of magazines and took out two pictures. One of me and Logan at last year's school prom, him in a tux two sizes too big, staring straight at the camera with a wide grin, me in a strapless baby blue satin dress with a white orchid corsage, which Logan had given me. I wasn't smiling effortlessly, like him.

The other picture was of me and Phoenix, taken in a booth, just head and shoulders. Phoenix struck an ironic pose, cool and beautiful. I had my cropped auburn hair and mascara eyes, and I was laughing.

End of story. There was Darina-pre-Phoenix and Darina-post-Phoenix—two different people, a new chemical mix, a white-hot fusion of souls.

And it was impossible to reverse the process, to clear up the misunderstandings and get back the communication I'd once had with Logan. Clearly he wanted more, anyway.

All Tuesday and Wednesday I avoided him and his secret, significant glances. As if I didn't already know it, the anniversary of Jonas's death was approaching fast and there was talk at school of some kind of memorial procession of Harleys, headed up by Matt Fortune of all people, on a bike provided by his brother, Charlie.

"We'll meet in town after school next Tuesday," Matt explained in the cafeteria to the familiar gang of boys, which included Christian and Lucas but not Logan. "We ride out through Centennial—slowly, at maybe ten miles per hour—and hold the same speed when we reach the Foxton highway. We stop at the exact spot where the crash happened."

"Creepy." Jordan backed out of the group and left the guys to their plans.

Hannah stuck around with me, a few tables away. "I don't know, maybe it's a good thing in a Gothic sort of way," she muttered.

"Or totally ghoulish." I poked at my drab food, not hungry at all. I couldn't decide either, only I found it interesting that Matt was right at the center of the plan.

"Cool!" Lucas got behind the idea. "I bet Jonas will be up there, looking down on us and giving his blessing."

I shuddered at the rose-tinted picture of angels floating on fluffy, floaty clouds, probably playing harps and surrounded by sunny peacefulness. *No,* I wanted to say, *it's not like that. It's dangerous, hard, and restless. A million winged souls are fighting to return.*

"Where will you get a bike?" Christian asked Lucas.

"Maybe Charlie has a spare. Can you ask him, Matt?"

"Do the girls get to ride with you?" Hannah didn't want to be left out. "I want to leave flowers by the roadside."

The plan was taking shape. Matt's next neat idea was that the slow procession should be led by Bob Jonson, with the kids Jonas's age following behind.

"Whoa, can he handle it?" Lucas asked. "I hear he's pretty shaky right now alone in the house. We don't want to push him too hard."

"At least give him the chance," Matt insisted, strutting his stuff in front of another couple of girls who'd been drawn in. "We'll be riding right behind him, remember."

"It's so cool!" one of the newcomers sighed, clearly hooked on Matt's idea and not caring in the least about Jonas. "The rest of us can line the route then drive out later to lay flowers."

"Maybe we should contact Zoey and ask her to come along," someone else suggested.

Flowers, Harleys, silent tributes at the roadside by people who couldn't care less…and now Zoey. To me this was turning into a crazy circus. "Jonas wasn't that sort of guy,"

I reminded them. "He wasn't into drama and making a big deal of things."

Matt turned on me. "Yeah, Darina, don't tell me. You knew Jonas way better than the rest of us. Go ahead, speak for him, why don't you?"

"I don't remember *you* being close with Jonas," I retaliated. "How come you're so into this procession thing?"

"What are you saying?" Matt broke away from the group and came right up to me, eyeball to eyeball. "That I'm faking? That I don't have any feelings for Jonas?"

"Do you?" I refused to look away, staring into Matt Fortune's weird flecked eyes, a mix of hazel and green, under heavy, straight brows.

Matt blinked and he turned away. "So about next Tuesday," he went on smoothly. "Who's going to ask Bob Jonson?"

"Dude, you do it," Christian spoke for the others. "Say it'll help bring closure, poor guy."

Matt waited until Thursday for payback. He cornered me as I was driving out of the school gates in my convertible, driving his flatbed truck alongside and forcing me onto the sidewalk outside the 7-Eleven.

"Nice car," he said, leaning across his passenger seat.

I was more than a little ticked off. "Are you crazy?" I barked. "What are you trying to do to me?"

"I hear it's a gift from Brandon Rohr."

"That's none of your business."

"And you're so good at keeping your nose out of other people's stuff." He sneered, jumping out of his truck and walking around to my window. "In the future you stay out of my face, you hear?"

"I'm not in your face." I was scared but I didn't show it.

"No? Didn't you come sneaking around to Charlie's place? Didn't you make me look small over next Tuesday's deal?"

I stared calmly from my driver's seat. "It's not difficult to make you look small, Matt."

"You're a real bitch, you know that?" His fist landed on my windshield, making a shopper exiting the store stare hard before she went on her way.

"I only wanted to know how come you were suddenly Jonas's buddy," I said, hammering the nail into his thick skull. "I remember the time, not too long ago, when you and he were fighting tooth and claw over Zoey."

Matt was tanned, strong, and healthy, so he didn't turn pale. But everything else about him registered shock. He kind of shrank back, then boosted himself up again, back to the guy who spent too much time in the gym. "That's crap," he told me. "Zoey and Jonas were the real thing, everybody knew."

"So, if you knew it, why try to get her back?"

"Says who?"

"Says Zoey." The more he toughed it out the calmer I grew. What was the worst that could happen? A fist through my shiny new windshield, Matt blowing off a whole lot more hot air.

"BS," he muttered.

Pushing the gear stick from Neutral into Drive, I got ready to coast away. But before I left, I wanted to give Matt plenty to think about. "Whose word do I take?" I asked him. "Yours or Zoey's?"

And I headed straight for the clinic in time to intercept Zoey as she came out of Kim Reiss's room.

"You two are good friends, huh?" Kim asked when she saw the greeting Zoey gave me.

Zoey had zoomed over to me in her wheelchair and grabbed me by both hands as I sat in Kim's waiting room. "Darina, I'm sorry about Sunday—about my dad," she'd said.

"Zoey and I go way back," I told Kim. "Can you give us five minutes?"

"Come in when you're ready," Kim replied, going back into her room and closing the door.

"How are you doing?" I asked. I'm not big on the healing power of hugs, but for Zoey I made an exception.

"Good."

"You've been crying?"

"Yeah, but positive crying," she said, trying to smile. "Kim says let the tears fall. I told her I remembered after the crash, lying on the road with Jonas hovering over me. She says that's good too. I told her you'd helped."

"Thanks." But I needed more, and I truly didn't have much time. "How about *before* the crash?"

Zoey shook her head. "My mind won't go there. I want it to, but every time I try, I hit a wall."

"Anything? Anything at all?"

She struggled again, closing her eyes and squeezing her temples with her long fingers. "Matt Fortune," she muttered.

The name sent my head spinning. "What about him?"

"I don't know. I keep seeing his face. I don't want to. I want to see Jonas. But Matt won't leave."

"When is this? How long before the accident? Is it the same day?"

Zoey let her hands fall into her lap. "No. It's maybe a week before. Yeah, Matt was hanging around, coming to my house, following me home from school."

"He was stalking you?" *More, Zoey, more!*

She nodded. "He was a pain in the butt, I remember. It's kind of hazy, but he would wait until Jonas wasn't around then he would act like we were still an item. I wasn't comfortable and told him to back off, even though I didn't want to hurt his feelings."

"Matt Fortune has a thick skin," I pointed out. "His feelings aren't easily hurt."

"Well, he didn't back off and things got kind of nasty when I finally mentioned it to Jonas. I was scared there was going to be a fight."

At that moment, Kim opened her door. "Darina, it's past four thirty. We're into your hour—the clock's ticking."

"OK, another minute," I told her.

Click went her door. "*Was* there a fight?" I asked Zoey.

She frowned. "No. At least, I don't remember one. All I get is Matt's face when I want Jonas's. Why is that?"

"I wish I knew. Go back to crash day. Focus on that."

"I tried to do that for Kim. I really tried," Zoey said. "All I get when I picture the Foxton road is a flash of light—no noise, no wheels spinning, no brakes, nothing. A flash and then darkness."

A flash of light. And Matt Fortune's face where she didn't want it to be. There had to be a connection between the two. But Mrs. Bishop was coming to fetch Zoey and my own hour was ticking. I squeezed Zoey's hand and went in to talk with Kim.

"I still see Phoenix all the time," I told my shrink. I figured it was best to tell the truth in here and let her draw her own conclusions. She wasn't allowed to tell anyone anything I said, anyway.

"And how does it make you feel?"

"Happy."

"And?"

"Sad, awful, chewed up, when I have to say good-bye."

"Describe Phoenix to me, Darina."

"He's the most beautiful thing you ever saw. Plus, he makes me laugh," I told her. "He has this crazy point of view. He jokes about things that people say are serious—politics, money, whatever. Then again, he's serious about the right stuff—telling it like it is, being honest. I love that about him."

There was no sunlight today in Kim's office. The sky outside was blue-gray, the color of a bruise, with a rim of bright gold around the edge of the heavy clouds.

"And more about his appearance?" she asked quietly.

"Every time I look at him I notice his eyes. Like I'm hypnotized."

"What color are his eyes?"

"Gray-blue. Shining. His skin's so clear."

Kim sat for a while, resting back in her soft taupe chair. "I notice something significant," she said at last.

I waited again. The hour was almost over. I'd said zilch

this session about the Beautiful Dead and I wondered how much my therapist had figured out.

"When I ask you to describe Phoenix, you talk about him in the present tense," she pointed out. "So much so that it's as if you almost feel him here in the room."

Right after my shrink session I switched off my phone and drove out to Foxton. Slow drops of rain splashed the windshield but I didn't bother to stop and put up the top. The cold wetness on my skin felt good.

I was driving fast into the mountains, into an approaching storm. Before I knew it I'd passed the spot where the road splits, keeping to the highway, not caring whether or not I was seen. Soon I reached the huddle of houses at the Foxton junction and turned left, past the rickety fishing lodges overlooking the clear green, fast running water of Foxton Creek.

The rain came down harder now, soaking my hair and my white T-shirt. *Stop and fix the top,* I told myself, but another impatient part of my brain said, *Don't waste time. Keep on driving.* Past the lodges and a Jeep driven by a solitary hunter who kept steadily to the speed limit. Through the trees ruined by a forest fire—black, twisted stumps and gray burned-out logs left to rot back into the earth. Then on up the incline into fresh, green aspens under the blue-black sky. One name was driving me on and making me desperate to see Jonas: Matt Fortune. He'd grown in my mind from a minor irritant into a major player in the mess that had ended in Jonas's tragic crash. If there were an answer, it lay with him.

Tell me about Matt. Zoey said you two almost had a fight. How jealous was he? Was he out of control? I put my foot on the pedal as I rehearsed the questions I'd ask Jonas and drove through the rain onto Foxton Ridge.

When I couldn't drive any farther, I finally put the top on, jumped out of the car, and ran through the long grass to the water tower. By this time I was soaked to the skin and shivering with cold—the only living thing out there in the storm, with the rain splattering against the rusted metal of the tower as background noise.

That's weird—there are no wings beating. I waited for Hunter to set up the barrier that drove unwelcome visitors away, but it didn't happen.

Where are you all? I stepped out from under the tower and began to walk down the hill.

Phoenix, it's me, Darina!

I hated the silence, longed to hear the spooky wings of the Beautiful Dead. Why hadn't their super-sharp hearing picked up the sound of my car engine or the swish of my footsteps through the grass?

"Phoenix?" I reached the side meadow and called his name out loud.

The barn door creaked then banged. Once, twice, three times. I walked inside and looked around. There were cobwebs in the rafters, dust on the floor, as if nothing had disturbed them in years. The old bridles and harnesses hung on their hooks, a rusty hay fork, an ax, and a shovel rested against a stall door. "Jonas! Summer! Is anyone around?"

My voice disturbed a small, scuttling creature in the hay loft above my head.

Bang! The wind in the door sent a strong shudder through my body.

I ran out of the barn, across the yard toward the house. The door was locked. "Let me in!" I yelled, rattling at the handle.

Outside the porch, the rain poured down. There was a flicker of lightning and then a low roll of thunder.

"Hunter, let me in!" I ran to the window and peered through a film of grime. The rocking chair, the stove, the table looked untouched, like a museum that had been closed for decades. Around the side of the house I found a rotting rain barrel and the shafts and base of an ancient wooden cart. I missed my footing and slipped down the slope toward the rushing creek, only saving myself by grabbing at the slim trunk of an aspen sapling. When I got my balance I started to cry.

Where has everyone gone? Please come back! Under the low clouds and pouring rain I wandered out into the yard, stepping through puddles and searching every corner of the deserted place. Another fork of lightning split the sky in half and the crash of thunder sent me running back to the barn.

Bang! *Suppose it never happened.*

Bang! *The Beautiful Dead don't exist.*

Bang! *Phoenix didn't come back. He's dead and gone forever.*

I sank to the floor and wept until I was exhausted. Then I thought it through and tried to deal with the shock of realizing that I was one crazy girl driven out of her head by the loss of the person in the world who had meant everything to her.

I said it out loud to teach myself the lesson. "Who else saw the Beautiful Dead, Darina? Sure, there were rumors. Everyone in Ellerton was shaken up by these four deaths, that was only to be expected. Scared minds invent stupid stuff—ghosts and supernatural noises that turn out to be the wind rustling through trees, period. And sure, I found Jonas's belt buckle, but what did that prove? Only that he was here some time before he died. What other so-called proof did I have?"

Phoenix's kisses, his eyes staring into mine, and an angel-wing tattoo.

175

My belief crumbled under the force of the storm and the eerie stillness of the barn. It ebbed out of me, leaving a hollow that was soon filled with a creeping sense of death and decay all around. Now the horse halters looked like hangman's nooses and the ax in the corner belonged to a masked executioner. The scuttling feet upstairs were rats ready to gnaw at dead flesh. Lightning struck again and thunder rattled and crashed down the valley. I sat on the barn floor wishing that the storm would gather me up and hurl me against the mountains, smashing me into a thousand pieces.

For a long time despair held me in its grip until the sky grew quieter and the clouds began to part. A crescent moon appeared—an arc of silver light—then tiny stars millions of light years away.

"Maybe there's a reason they had to leave," I murmured, raising myself up and shuffling to the door to gaze at the heavens. "Phoenix was here for a short while, along with Hunter and the others. The Beautiful Dead did exist."

A wind carried the clouds in the direction of Amos Peak and now the night sky seemed huge, the Milky Way a curving stream of pale light against the sparkling blackness. The world was a tiny speck in the unknowable universe. Which made me smaller than a single atom in the grand scheme, my sorrows invisible.

I saw a shooting star dart across the darkness, then flare and fade. Another one made its spectacular descent, then another and another. Four in quick succession—Jonas, Arizona, Summer, and Phoenix shining bright and dying.

Tears filled my eyes.

At dawn there was not a cloud in the sky, only a pink light in the east and a golden sun rising clear of Amos Peak.

8

With the rising sun I felt hope, and I grew more certain that Phoenix would never leave me without saying good-bye.

This hope replaced the panic of the night before, when the storm was at its height. It filled me with warmth, so that I could walk out through the wide door and calmly breathe the fresh morning air. I noticed the house, battered but watertight, then spotted a rain-soaked coyote slink out from under the rusted truck where it had taken shelter during the storm. In the air all around was the lovely, sighing sound of wind rustling through the aspens. When I turned back toward the barn, I saw the Beautiful Dead.

"Together we are strong," they murmured, hands clasped, the men naked to the waist and all standing in a tight circle inside the barn. Hunter the overlord stood in the middle of the circle, head bowed, hands clasped in front of him.

"We are stronger than the warring heavens." He led the

chant while the others followed, like priest and congregation. "Stronger than the light that splits the sky. We, the Beautiful Dead, rejoice in our strength."

My gaze was drawn to Phoenix. He was taller than any of them, and the most beautiful of all, even turned away from me and facing in toward Hunter, following his words. I saw his broad shoulders and the death mark between his shoulder blades where the knife had entered. I was filled with overwhelming love.

"Come and join us, Darina," Hunter said, raising his head and looking at me without surprise.

Phoenix turned and opened his arms. I ran to him, flooded with relief. He held me close, my head against his chest.

"You know I wouldn't leave you," he whispered, breathing into my hair.

I tilted my head to look into his eyes and nodded "I know it. But what happened? Was it the storm?"

"The force of the charge in an electrical storm is too strong," Phoenix told me, his musical voice deep. "It takes our powers away."

"So where did you go?" Slowly I was releasing my hold and trying to disguise my joyous relief from the others—Arizona especially, with her patronizing stare. I made out like I knew they'd be back all along.

"A lightning storm forces us back into limbo," Jonas explained. "We retreat from the far side until it passes."

"What happens if you don't?" It wasn't until I'd asked my hasty question that I realized they were unsettled. Summer stared unhappily at the ground, while Donna, Eve, and Iceman turned away from the circle.

Hunter took charge. "Like Phoenix said, our powers disappear," he said firmly. "And they don't return. If we're caught here in a lightning storm, we must stay forever on the far side."

This was news to me and I eagerly took hold of Phoenix's hand. "Why didn't you tell me? That means you could stay here with me—"

"Me, me, me!" Arizona piped scornfully. "Tell her the rest, Phoenix."

"We lose our power and are condemned to stay," he confirmed, trying not to look me in the eye.

"'Condemned'—how?" Why was this so bad, given that he loved me and I loved him? I looked into his eyes and saw a barrier that made me suspect that this time Phoenix didn't want to share the truth with me.

"As soon as we lose our power to return to limbo, stuff begins to happen," he muttered.

"What stuff?" I noticed that Summer and Jonas had also faded from the circle. Only Arizona and Hunter had stayed to listen.

A deep frown appeared on Phoenix's face. "If we get trapped here, we can't regenerate."

It took awhile for me to grasp what he was saying then I gave a small gasp.

"We're dead, remember." Trust Arizona to zap it to me.

"A dead person trapped on the far side after an electrical storm doesn't last long. Maybe a week, if that."

Now I wished I could turn the clock back two minutes to the point before I began to ask questions, when all I felt was relief in Phoenix's arms. A chill entered my heart and I shuddered.

"We start to decompose from day one," merciless Arizona went on. "Our eyes cloud over and we turn blind. Our joints decay, we move more slowly."

"Don't," I pleaded. "I get it."

"You wanted to know," she insisted. "Day two, open wounds begin to rot."

"Enough, Arizona." Hunter stepped forward. "That's where the far side gets its image of us from," he explained to me in a voice that seemed less harsh than before. "The mindless monster that thrives on human flesh. But don't worry, Darina, I take good care of my charges. I won't let it happen to them."

Catching my breath, I nodded at him. The picture Arizona had painted revolted me and images from horror movies crowded into my head. "You'll look out for Phoenix?" I begged Hunter.

"I swear," he promised. "You see how I protected him during last night's storm."

"Thank you. Believe me—thank you." It was fall, the time of year when storms hit, when hot air blows up from the Gulf of Mexico and clashes with the cold air of the mountains. I knew that before long it would happen again.

Hunter looked at me calmly before he unhitched his gray shirt from the waistband of his black jeans and put it on. Then he, Phoenix, and Jonas drew me to one side. "You brought us some news," Hunter said.

"About Matt Fortune," I told them, fixing my mind on my last conversation with Zoey. "Zoey said that Matt was fighting with Jonas, trying to get her back." I turned to Jonas. "Is that how you remember it?"

He nodded. "Matt did try to screw things up a couple of times. He acted like he could walk back into her life whenever he wanted. That's the way he is. I didn't pay a whole lot of attention."

"Because you and Zoey had really clicked and you knew he was no threat." To me this fitted the picture I already had. "Is it true Matt tried to draw you into a fight?"

Another nod from Jonas, while Hunter and Phoenix both

listened more intently than the others. "I was getting my bike fixed. We were standing outside Charlie's place when he threw a punch. But I'm not the fighting kind."

"What did you do?"

"I ducked. Matt swung his fist so hard he overbalanced against his Tourer, sent it crashing down. Charlie heard the noise and rushed out of his workshop. I got on my bike and rode away, end of story."

"One dented Harley and one bruised ego," Phoenix remarked to Hunter.

"But listen, there's more." Zoey's words were flooding back now. "Whenever Zoey tries to recall the day of the crash, there's a block on the actual details and it's Matt Fortune's face she sees. In among all that pain and trauma, he's there and he won't go away."

"Does she know why?" Phoenix asked me.

I shook my head. "She tries so hard to get rid of his face, but it doesn't happen. It drives her crazy."

"I don't like this," Jonas said darkly. "I said go easy on Zoey, remember."

Now Jonas was sounding like Zoey's parents, but in his case I could totally understand. "You want me to back off?" Four days before his twelve months were up.

There was a long silence and it felt like we'd hit a wall until Summer came over and put her arm around Jonas's shoulder. "Stay strong," she told him. "The truth's going to hurt—we always knew that."

I hadn't expected this from Summer—she seemed to bend too easily, like the silvery grass around us; she was too gentle to take this line. Then again, the Beautiful Dead had all put their faith in me and wanted me to succeed.

"I'm sorry," I told Jonas. "I only talked with Zoey about the stuff she discusses with her shrink. I guess she'd be hurting anyway."

"And if Zoey is in too much pain right now, we should turn our attention to Matt Fortune," Hunter decided, looking ahead. "That is, if we believe he played a role in this."

I thought for a while. "My gut tells me, yes, he did. I don't have the exact facts, but there's something about Matt—the way he's so hostile when I ask questions. And now he's planning a big memorial procession for Tuesday, which is so not like him…"

"Stop. Tell us about this," Hunter insisted.

I told them about the slow ride out of town through Centennial to the fatal spot under the neon cross. And how they planned to include Jonas's father and the girls laying flowers, the whole deal.

Jonas lowered his head to the ground. He closed his eyes. "Keep Zoey out of it," he pleaded.

"No problem. Her folks won't let her anywhere near it." That, I was one hundred percent sure of.

"Hey, Darina, does Jonas really need to know about this big procession?" Arizona interrupted. "Imagine how he feels right now. It's way worse than reading your own obituary."

Hunter pulled us back on track. "Let's focus on Matt. Darina, is there any way you can get the truth out of this guy?"

"Without getting into stuff you can't handle?" Phoenix added. He stood next to me, face-to-face with Summer and Jonas.

"I know—why not drag the cops in, tell them you suspect Matt?" Arizona knew her suggestion was off the wall; it was her way of rubbing my nose in the dirt. "Say, 'Hey, Sheriff, you got it all wrong. Jonas Jonson didn't kill himself and maim his girlfriend. It was all because of Matt Fortune!' 'Give me the proof,' grunts the officer. 'Why, Sheriff, it's my gut telling me he's guilty. I didn't realize you needed proof!'"

"Arizona, back off." It was the first time I'd seen Hunter show a flicker of true annoyance with her. "I'm warning you, OK?"

"No problem, I can take it," I told him. "Anyway, Arizona's right. I know the official version of the incident will be hard to break down. The inquest gave everyone neat answers, and that's the version they'll hold on to."

"Everyone except Jonas's dad," Hunter pointed out. "He's not into easy solutions—he knows there's more."

"I want you all to back off," Jonas broke in. His face was drained, his eyes tormented. "What we're doing here, it's not right. I'm hurting the people I love."

Summer sensed his agony and held his hand tight. She knew enough about how he was feeling not to contradict him.

"Zoey and your dad are hurting anyway," Hunter said after a long silence. "But you do have a choice here, Jonas. You can drop this whole thing if that's what you want. Is it?"

I stared at Jonas's suffering face, biting my lip and waiting for his answer.

"And then what?" Arizona asked, her voice soft and hardly recognizable. "You drop it now and it's the end. You never get a second chance."

And the truth dies with you, I thought. I wanted Jonas to fight on and not give in. "Zoey's stronger than you think," I murmured. "People are."

He looked up at me, his eyelids flickering.

"She needs to know," I insisted.

Jonas blinked and nodded.

"Is that a yes?" Arizona asked.

He didn't answer. He didn't have to.

"Promise not to do anything stupid," Phoenix insisted as we reached my new red convertible. The roof was up, but the leather seats were still soaked by the night's rain now steaming gently under the morning sun.

"Are you listening, Darina? Don't put Matt under pressure—not face-to-face. It's too risky."

I reached out for him and kissed him, tingling at the feel of his soft, cool lips, sighing at the indescribable surge of emotion I felt. My heart was on fire. I was a happy mess, in spite of all the confusion and horror and mystery that swirled around me. Close up, his features blurred through the flickering fringe of my lashes, but his eyes shone clear into mine.

"Nothing stupid, OK?" he murmured.

"Don't speak," I begged. We'd come to the parting bit again and I was putting it off, greedy for more time.

"I won't be able to rest until this is over," he murmured.

"So what's new? I guess the Beautiful Dead never sleep anyway," I whispered back.

"Right. We don't." He pulled away at last. "Brandon sure knows how to pick a car." He grinned, patting the car windshield and dragging me back into the real world.

"You know I like it," I reminded him. "But I haven't worked out my official story yet. Like, why did Brandon Rohr give me a shiny red convertible?"

"Keep people guessing." Phoenix held on to my hand as

I searched with the other for my car key. "And remember, Brandon's there for you if you need him."

I pulled the key from my jeans pocket. "I'll remember that when Laura rips me to pieces for staying out all night."

"Will she think the worst?" He was still grinning, turning a little bit sheepish but also amused.

"Well, she can't think I spent the night with you!" I joked back. Behind the kidding around, my heartstrings were stretched to breaking point. "I've got to go," I whispered.

He embraced me one more time.

"I'm there for you too," he whispered. "Even though you don't always see me."

"Trust me," I told him. "Remember that I love you and no one else."

"I was at Jordan's place," I told Laura. "What's the big deal?"

She'd stayed home from work, crazy with worry, calling practically every number in the Ellerton phone book.

"Darina, you don't stay out all night without telling me!"

"Sorry."

"Why didn't you call?"

"My phone was out of minutes. I forgot."

"I thought you'd had an accident. That car's way too powerful. And then the storm. Jim and I sat up all night waiting for them to come and tell us you'd driven off the road."

"I said I was sorry, OK?" I had to change my clothes and get to school. I had to see Matt. "Give me a break, will you? I'm fine."

Laura was too wound up to hear me. "I even called the Rohrs' place. I asked if you were with Brandon."

"Puh-lease!" Disappearing into my bedroom, I shut the door behind me.

"What am I supposed to think?" she yelled. "His brother is…" Her voice caught. "Let me just put it this way: The guy brings you a convertible and it's not even your birthday!"

It was so weird being in school, doing normal stuff. The teachers asked me for work I hadn't done, my math teacher checked me out to make sure I wasn't going to pass out in her class again. My friends pussyfooted around me.

"Check out Darina's car," Hannah cooed as we left the building after last period with Jordan and Lucas in tow. Jordan had the hots for Lucas but he wasn't interested. That was another story. Frankly, given everything else that was going on, a simple unrequited crush would have been a nice distraction. But I had to stay focused.

"How did you pay for that?" Lucas whistled through his teeth when he saw the convertible.

"Can we get a ride?" Jordan asked.

I stood back, welcoming the attention for once. I

knew it wouldn't be long before Matt Fortune came sniffing around.

Sure enough, he joined the group with Logan and Christian, overlooking the fight we'd had outside the 7-Eleven and pretending that he knew all there was to know about every shiny nut and bolt, every piston, spark plug, and gasket in the engine of my mean machine. Guy stuff.

"Jump in, let's take a ride," I said to him. I included Logan in the offer, so the others didn't get the wrong idea about me and Matt. I planned to drop Logan off at his house and drive on into town with Matt.

They didn't wait to be asked twice and moments later I was driving the two of them down the road, leaving Jordan, Hannah, Christian, and Lucas staring. I'd told Jordan the lurid details about Matt forcing me up onto the sidewalk, so her jaw hung lower than the rest. Not to mention that I'd just snatched Logan away from her.

Matt sat in the front passenger seat, lolling against the headrest. Logan said nothing. I guess he was wondering why I'd invited Matt too.

"How are the plans for Tuesday?" I asked as we stopped at a red light.

"Good." Matt looked sideways at me without moving his head.

"Sorry I gave you a hard time." *Say it like you mean it,* I told myself. *Remember what you learned in those after-school acting classes.*

"Does that mean you'll be there?" he wanted to know.

"Count me in, red roses and all. What about you, Logan?" I glanced in my mirror.

"Sure, I'll be there with Lucas."

"Cool. Did Charlie give you and Lucas Harleys for the day?" My question was to Logan, but Matt jumped in with the answer.

"Charlie thinks it's a great idea. A whole town thing, a big Ellerton event. So, yeah, he'll provide the bikes."

My plan was to keep Matt at the focus of this conversation, and it was working like a dream. "And did you ask Bob Jonson to lead us? What did he say?"

"It broke him up. He cried right in front of me."

"The guy isn't doing well," Logan muttered from the backseat.

"Yeah, but he sucked it up," Matt went on. By this time he had his feet up on my control console and his right arm was hanging over the side of the car. "He said he'd be honored to lead the procession. Honored."

I turned down a side street and pulled up outside Logan's house. His dad was sitting in the porch drinking beer with none other than Bob Jonson.

"Hey, Bob!" Matt called, lazily raising his arm in a half wave.

I watched Logan's face in the mirror as he got out of the car, like he'd swallowed a lemon. He walked away without saying good-bye.

"Hey, Matt." Bob returned the wave by raising a bottle to him—a slow, clumsy movement.

"Smashed again," Matt grunted then told me to drive off fast, before Bob had a chance to stagger down the steps toward us. "The question is—will he sober up by Tuesday?"

I drove on into town, trying to handle my dislike of the guy sitting next to me, relying on his vanity to get me where I needed to be. "How about a coffee?" I asked, turning in the direction of the mall.

"Are you for real?"

I gave him a pouty smile and fluffed up my hair. "Since when did you turn down this kind of offer?"

He laughed. "So, Darina, when did you stop hating me?"

"Hey, Matt, I never hated you," I lied. *Get a load of this, any talent scouts out there.* "It's just that I've been going through a rough time."

"With Phoenix and all," he said.

Yeah, that. "I got closure on it after the funeral, but it took a while." I glanced at him, slouched beside me, the wind whipping through his hair. His guard was down, but I still needed to go really slow. "I guess I acted kind of crazy."

192

"Show me a girl who isn't." He shrugged. "Are you still talking with Zoey?"

"No way." *Try a wry smile, another shrug.* "She's even more nuts than I am."

"In what way?" The guard was halfway back up. He shifted in the seat, looking at me from under heavy, furrowed brows.

"Saying all kinds of stuff."

"Like what?"

"Like, she could see Jonas looking down on her, asking if she was OK, when everyone knows he died on the spot. I told her it was part of the PTSD syndrome."

Matt's blank eyes told me that he had no clue what this meant.

"Post-traumatic stress disorder," I explained. "Zoey's brains are cooked. She has no memory of what really happened."

His guard dropped again. "Let's not talk about Zoey," he said, cozying up to me. "Darina, I've forgotten how cool you can be, you know that?"

This was where the eyelash flutter came in, and more pouting. No words. It turns out I deserved an Oscar.

"You think out of the box," he went on. "I like that about you. Not like Zoey."

"I thought we weren't talking about her." Less than twelve hours ago I'd been with Phoenix. Now here I was with Matt Fortune, trying not to feel nauseated.

"Right. Zoey had her chance and she blew it." His arm was resting along the back of the seat, his hand creeping onto my bare shoulder. "So how come you played hard to get way back then?"

I chose not to waste my breath by going into the issue of loyalty between friends. "You want the truth?" I simpered. "I didn't take you seriously, Matt. I thought you were out of my league."

Matt Fortune was immune to irony. Maybe his mom had vaccinated him against it, along with rubella and chicken pox. His hand was definitely resting on my shoulder now. I pulled up to the curb and jerked the car to a halt, half a block from the mall. The sidewalk was crowded with the after-school crowd.

"Anyway, I didn't want to get hurt. I thought you and Zoey would get back together."

"She was crazy even then," he confided, leaning in more closely. "It's not like I didn't offer to get back with her..." He suddenly seemed to realize we'd stopped moving. "Hey, I thought we were going for coffee."

"In a minute," I murmured softly. "So how much time did you waste on her?"

"Too long, hanging around her place, telling her Jonas was a loser."

"Yeah, loser." *Don't say too much, don't push too hard.*

"Maybe it was Jonas's Dyna that did it for Zoey."

"Maybe. He was such a loser!" Matt snorted and rested back against the seat. "The Dyna comes nowhere near the Tourer FLXH. The Street Glide—now there's a motorcycle!"

That was it—I'd found a solitary emotion lurking in his dark heart. Jealousy. Now I could safely stir it. "Jonas never looked cool on that bike. He wasn't born to ride."

"Tell me! The guy was an amateur. You put Jonas Jonson and me in a competition and I'd outride him every time."

I held my breath. "Did you ever do it—race him, I mean? Did you win?"

"What do you think? Face it—am I going to admit it to you, even if I did?"

"Oh, I get it—it's illegal." *Reel him in, slowly, slowly. Accept the dirty hand creeping along my collarbone.* "You're talking speed limits and crap like that. So, did you anyway?"

Slow thoughts clunked through Matt's brain, flashing up a security alert. High risk. Delete.

"Don't answer that." I laughed. But it was too late.

Matt jerked back so suddenly that his elbow slammed against the passenger door. "You don't trap me that way, you little bitch."

Whoa. He was practically screaming. Kids on the sidewalk flashed a few puzzled stares. "Get the hell out of here," Matt snarled, somehow forgetting he was in my car.

Jealousy…and now raw anger—so not attractive. My pulse picked up a notch. How could I throw him out of the car? I wished it had an eject button…"You nasty, little slut," he hissed. "To think that I would even…"

Something cut him off in mid-sentence: namely the two burly hands of Brandon Rohr. One had thrown open the door; the other had grabbed Matt by the collar of his stupid leather jacket. He flung Matt out onto the sidewalk as if he were a side of meat and slammed the door shut.

"You even touch her and you're dead!" Brandon yelled and the whole world heard.

And now Matt didn't look strong, he didn't look cool either.

He was a puppet dangling in Brandon's grasp, pressed up against a shop window, unable to say a word.

It was way past time to ask myself some basic questions. *Am I out of my depth, not waving but drowning? Have I messed up so badly that now I'll never be able to get the answers to Jonas's questions?*

Midnight is the hour for losing your nerve, especially after the latest fight I'd had with Laura two hours earlier.

"What happened to us, Darina?…We were so close… When did the whole thing fall apart?" *Boo-hoo, I'm dying here.*

I was still shaking from the Matt Fortune episode so I let

her get to me. I was crying too and saying sorry and then Laura was saying sorry and we ended up clinging to each other and promising to try harder on both sides. She went out happy to a late night movie. I felt crappy.

Darina, you did this all wrong, I told myself in the darkness of my room. *You made an enemy out of Matt Fortune. You thought you were smarter and stronger than you are. You think you can handle communing with dead people, for God's sake!*

I was even asking myself whether it would have worked out better if I'd never heard the barn door banging out at Foxton, and never found Phoenix again. I pulled the pillow over my face, trying but failing to block out that stupid question. When I pushed it off again, I felt someone else in the room.

"Who is it?" I whispered.

Shadows moved along the walls. There was no sound, only the sense of quiet breathing and eyes watching. Maybe wings beating softly—I couldn't be sure.

"Phoenix, is it you?"

"Do you want me to leave?" he asked.

I could hear him but not see him. "So now what—you're reading my mind?"

"Yes," he admitted. "If you want me to, I can go and never come back."

"Phoenix Rohr, don't you dare." I jumped off the bed and switched on the light. "You materialize, or whatever it is you do, right here, right now."

I was looking in the wrong direction when it started to happen, so when I turned toward the door I saw a shimmery outline gradually filling in with detail—Phoenix's lean body, his pale face and dark hair, and at last those all-seeing gray-blue eyes.

"Do you really wish you'd never found me again?" was his first, hurt question.

I'd never seen him like this—doubtful and holding back until I set his mind at rest.

"Me and my lousy thoughts," I sighed. "I was lying alone in the dark. I was like a scared kid, that's all."

Phoenix shook his head and stayed by the door. "I can understand if you did."

"No. I was feeling crappy. I didn't mean it." *Please believe me. If you're reading my thoughts right now, believe them.*

"Darina, you've done so much already. But you still have a choice. If you wanted to step away now, no one would blame you. Hunter will come if I call him. He's given the order that he's the only one who can do the memory thing on you. He'd do it and you'd forget all about us."

Now I was really afraid—not little-kid-in-the-middle-of-the-night scared. My heart was hammering against my rib cage. "And then what? How would Jonas get where he wants to be? He only has till Tuesday."

"That's not your problem." Finally Phoenix came toward me and took both my hands. "If Hunter works on you, you won't feel bad. And, like I told you before, you'll still have those great memories of you and me before..." He faltered, looking so grave and gentle, his hands trembling as they held mine.

I looked deep into his eyes. "OK, Mister Mind Reader, what do you see?"

I want to be with you. I never want to leave you. What you say about love is true. It's in everything we touch and see. Stay with me.

Slowly a smile appeared on Phoenix's face and a light came into his eyes. "I understand," he said.

9

We sat on my bed, Phoenix and I, and there was no need to talk.

"Did you finally learn how to stop the world?" I asked at last.

"Would you like me to?"

"Yes."

"One stationary world coming up." He grinned and snapped his fingers.

"Make that with fries, no mayo." We fell back laughing. In his arms, under his loving protection, I finally felt safe. At least for the moment.

"So, Brandon did his tough guy thing," I told Phoenix, snuggled face-to-face, limbs intertwined. "I guess you saw what happened at the diner?"

Phoenix let go of me and lay on his back, one arm behind his head. "That's what Brandon does."

"Was that how come he ended up in jail?" I'd always been curious about this, but a criminal record is like an embarrassing illness—if you're polite and well behaved you don't ask. Now though, I wanted to know a little more.

Phoenix gazed at my ceiling. "Yeah, something like that."

"For fighting?"

"When he was still at school, he got way out of line—with Mom, with his teachers—usually just kidding around. But by the time he left, he was angry."

"What changed?"

Phoenix shifted position, both hands behind his head. "Brandon grew up, or he didn't, depending on how you look at it. He was strong physically and he had a short fuse. A couple of guys got him wound up over a girl, lying and saying he was a cradle snatcher, that she was underage. He snapped."

"A girl?" I wasn't expecting this. "I only ever see Brandon hanging out with guys."

"That's the reason." Phoenix half smiled. "Currently, in his mind, girls equal trouble. Mess with them and you end up in a correctional facility for nine months."

"Whereas, if you mess with guys, you make sure you have bigger muscles and it all works out." I got the picture. "Whatever. One thing's for sure—he's living up to his promise."

"To take care of you." Phoenix rolled back toward me, leaning on one elbow and gazing at me. "I need you to promise me something."

"Sure."

"If you still want to be in on the deal, don't trust Matt Fortune. Stay totally away from him, OK?"

"Sure." Nothing easier. "He's a jerk," I muttered through gritted teeth. "He doesn't have much of a brain, but enough to see where I was leading, at which point his guilty conscience kicked in and he lost control."

Phoenix frowned. "Did you learn anything new?"

I nodded. "He wouldn't admit it, but I think he raced Jonas on his Harley—maybe to make himself look good in front of Zoey."

Phoenix waited for more, looking at me as if he could sift through my jumbled thoughts and catalog them into alphabetical order, which I guess he really could.

"I put the race thing to him as an idea and it pushed his buttons," I explained. "That's why he'll never trust me again."

"That and Brandon."

"Which leaves us nowhere," I sighed. "Except, I got home with Matt Fortune's paw prints all over me and I had to jump in the shower."

"Sorry," Phoenix said again. And we were silent, just holding each other, until the front door clicked and Laura walked in with Jim.

I heard their relaxed voices, plus sounds that meant they were making a hot drink in the kitchen, with Jim saying the coffee would keep them awake and Laura saying that staying awake seemed like a good idea, then laughing.

"We have to keep our voices down," I warned Phoenix. "You can hear how thin these walls are."

"I have something important to tell you," he whispered, sitting up on the bed and swinging his legs over the side. I sat next to him. "Hunter has a new plan."

"Good. Because I don't." I'd been hitting my head against a wall when Phoenix appeared, after all.

Letting his clasped hands hang between his knees, Phoenix thought long and hard. "Maybe good, maybe bad," he warned quietly. "This new plan—he's keeping it from us. I think it's so we don't discuss it until he's ready."

"Yeah, Hunter's a true democrat."

"He's the overlord. He wants to see you," Phoenix told me uneasily. "Tomorrow—early."

"I'll be there," I agreed. I was scared, but this was Phoenix. There was no hesitation.

Laura and Jim came upstairs. It was time for Phoenix to leave. He kissed me hard on the lips then stepped back and went into himself, turning his concentration inward—it's hard to say exactly how. Only I knew he was still visible but his mind had gone, and soon the shimmering thing happened again, and I lost the details as a haze gathered and the wings fluttered, until he dissolved and the room was empty.

There was no chance of sleeping after that.

I lay awake and focused on the night life outside my window—black squirrels scrabbling over the roof, redwood boughs creaking. At dawn a pair of blue jays settled on the porch rail below.

I got dressed quietly and waited for Jim to drive Laura to the store—my only way of getting out of the house without having to answer the usual questions and run the risk of either of them picking up the fact that I was extra jumpy this morning. No way could I deal with the third degree.

Honestly, I was so nervous I couldn't make my fingers fasten my shirt buttons or zip up my plaid skirt. But once finished, I made my escape in the convertible. Shaky relief flowed in a sigh out of my lungs. I thought I was clear until halfway down my street, when Logan stepped out from behind the open trunk of his car.

"Why so early?" he asked in a cheery, neighborly way. Sometimes Logan Lavelle is seventeen going on seventy.

I had to brake hard to avoid him. "Logan, I could've run you down!" I yelled. *Not now, Logan, please!*

"Don't you know it's Saturday? No school."

"Ha-ha. So I'm up early. So what?"

"No, it's good," he said, wiping his hands on an old towel

then throwing it in the trunk. "I need a ride into town to buy oil for the engine."

I groaned inwardly. Hunter, the overlord of the Beautiful Dead had summoned me, and here I was, involved in grease and motor oil. But it was easier to say the usual yes to Logan than a suspicion-arousing no. "Jump in," I told him.

"Did you do that science homework? And did you know Lucas finally agreed to date Jordan?" It was the old Logan, running on like a train, talking about nothing. It felt a whole hell of a lot better than talking about the quality of our relationship, though, and how Logan wanted more. "And guess what—Bob Jonson was here at my house until two a.m. I thought he was never going to leave."

"Were he and your dad drinking all that time?" I figured best to keep up the chitchat: it was a short run into town and it wasn't taking me out of my way through Centennial.

"Pretty much. My dad can hold his liquor but not Bob. They had to call a taxi to take him home."

"That's not nice," I muttered. I pulled into the gas station up on the right. "Here you go," I said.

Logan ignored my cue for him to leave. "The poor guy couldn't stand up. They sat right under my window, drinking, talking, drinking. It was all about Jonas."

"Poor guy," I echoed. *I need to go, Logan. Get out of the car!*

"And stuff about Foxton," Logan went on. Which is when

I began to suspect an ulterior motive on his part. Logan studied my face closely. "It didn't make much sense, but Bob's convinced he can find Jonas up there on the ridge. He swears he's seen him."

"How drunk was he?" I muttered, pressing the button to unlock Logan's door. No way was he about to draw me in.

Logan's stubborn streak came into play. "Maybe there's something in it. Bob Jonson would stake his life on it."

"My shrink says that's what we do—we imagine seeing people we've just lost. They pop up and we think they're real flesh and blood. Sometimes we even talk with them." Amazingly, just as it had in Kim Reiss's office, it felt good to tell the truth.

"Shrink?" This was the first Logan had heard of it. I'd intended for him to be shocked, to sidetrack him, and then to hustle him out of the car.

I nodded. "It was Laura's idea. Because of Phoenix. Who'd have thought it—that she'd pay out for therapy?"

"Darina, I had no idea."

"The point is, people with PTSD imagine things, and that's what Jonas's dad is doing. He doesn't need alcohol, he needs help."

"Suppose it's true," Logan insisted, leaning back in his seat and turning his head toward me. Now he was definitely testing my reactions. "Suppose Jonas isn't really dead."

I shivered. "Logan, they buried him, remember? There was an autopsy—everything!"

He took a deep breath. "So what do you think is happening up there? Do we really have to start believing in ghosts?"

I closed my eyes. "Believe what you like, Logan. I have to go."

"To Foxton?" he muttered under his breath.

I slammed my hand on the rim of the steering wheel. "What did you say?"

"Forget it. You spend a lot of time up there, that's all."

"How do you know? Are you following me?"

"Why are you mad at me, Darina? I don't get it."

"I'm not mad," I yelled. "Logan, do you want to buy engine oil or not?"

He made another tactical swerve, "Since Phoenix died, you act like you hate all guys. You push me away, and you've known me all your life. You say something to Matt that turns him crazy—yeah, I heard about that."

"*I* said something to *Matt!* Exactly! It had nothing to do with *you!*" Now I was practically screaming. "You know something? This town sucks! You only have to breathe and someone is spreading bad rumors about you. Get out of my car, Logan. Now!"

His face looked stunned as he registered what I'd said. "I'm sorry, Darina—I didn't mean…"

I breathed out heavily. "So what did you mean, Logan? Let me tell you something—Matt Fortune jumped on me and Brandon Rohr saved me. End of story."

"Brandon Rohr." Logan picked up a different trail. His eyes went back to being angry.

"What do two and two make these days?" I shouted. This time I leaned over and opened the door myself. "It's five, isn't it? Get out, Logan. Just get out!"

I drove out to Foxton expecting another storm. The clouds over Amos Peak were so gray and bruised that I could almost smell thunder in the air.

"Not now," I said out loud, swinging off the highway at Foxton and heading along the side of the rushing creek. "I have an appointment with an undead overlord, so enough with the electric storms already." I was hoping to make myself laugh. I didn't.

A gray-haired woman sitting on the porch of one of the fishing shacks watched vacantly as I drove by. Maybe my car was the only one she'd seen all morning.

Then I was out of civilization, kicking up dust along the dirt track, swerving close to the edge and looking down on a mess of boulders, sparsely scattered with pines that had been twisted and blackened by the forest fire. Spots of heavy rain hit my windshield. Two mule deer broke cover from a willow thicket, springing across the track and disappearing down a gully. I bumped and rattled on into the mountains.

"Give me ten minutes with Hunter," I begged the sky. "No electric storm until he's told me his new plan."

The sky seemed to hear me. The rain stopped falling. But the mugginess hung thick in the air, suffocating me.

"Thanks," I muttered, pulling off the track and leaping out of the car.

Right away, before I'd even reached the top of the ridge, I felt the force field around the house of the Beautiful Dead. Those pulsating wings, millions of restless souls— where once they filled me with dread, now they made me glad, and I ran on as far as the water tower before I stopped for breath.

I dragged air into my lungs, staring down into the valley, hoping that it was Phoenix who would meet me and take me to Hunter.

But it was Iceman, whom I hardly knew. He strode up the hill to the sound of unseen creatures fluttering and hovering, his tense gaze fixed on me.

"Hunter's waiting," he said.

I came out from the shadow of the water tank. "Is everything OK?"

He nodded. "For as long as the storm holds off. Phoenix

and Arizona are checking the weather out by Amos Peak. Hunter's in the house."

Together Iceman and I ran down the slope. Though he was short, he was lithe—faster than me by far. He stopped by the mended fence until I caught up.

"Sorry," I muttered. "Lungs—legs—no good."

"You all right?" he checked.

"Yeah, go ahead." We jogged the last few hundred yards until we came to the house.

There, beside the old truck, with Hunter waiting for me inside, I had a sudden attack of nerves. I looked at Iceman. "Are you coming in with me?"

"No. Hunter said for you to go in alone."

"And what Hunter says we do," I acknowledged, stepping up onto the porch with a fluttering stomach and racing heart. Stupid me: I almost knocked on the door.

"Come in, Darina," Hunter said before I had the chance.

I turned the handle and stepped into whatever waited for me.

Hunter sat in the chair by the stove, his back turned, his long gray hair loose over his collar. Slowly he turned his head and I saw his chiseled features in profile—strong brow, nose, and jaw, pronounced cheekbones, hair swept back, with the blurred, faded death mark on his temple. Deliberately, it seemed, he didn't look at me.

I moved forward into the room and waited. I noticed the layers of dust on the table, the cracks in the green plates on the shelf. Hunter's history.

After maybe two minutes, still without speaking, he turned to face me. He gazed at my face like he was studying a map—the contours, the shaded areas, the shape of my lips, and the color of my eyes.

I was deafened by the silence, choked by the hundred years of dust. "Phoenix said you have a plan," I croaked.

Hunter stood up and towered over me. "Are you strong enough?" he wondered out loud.

I didn't flinch, even though he could hear my heart hammering. I met his gray gaze. "Try me."

"Can you endure pain?"

I took a sharp breath but didn't answer.

"You don't know yet—you're young."

"I lost Phoenix," I reminded him. "Do you mean worse pain than that?"

"Stand in the light," he ordered. "Over there by the window."

I did as he said, wondering if this was the room where Hunter had been shot all those years ago. Maybe there was dried blood on the floor. I let my gaze wander.

"No, Mentone didn't shoot me here. It was out on the porch," he told me in a clear voice.

I jumped and closed my eyes. *Damn it!*

"Marie didn't see it happen. She was here in the house. Don't tell me you're sorry."

"I wouldn't do that." I opened my eyes with a sigh.

"Why do you wear your hair short?" Hunter suddenly asked.

The personal question threw me almost more than anything else. "To be different," I whispered.

"Oh, Darina, you're different for sure," he said, smiling as if I had amused him. "I'm going to take a risk," he decided. "I've watched your dealings with Matt Fortune—a little clumsy at times, as Arizona predicted. But gutsy."

"Thanks. I think." The thudding at my ribs was lessening. I was able to breathe.

"The question is—is Matt the right guy?"

"Of course he is!" I cried, forgetting to be scared. "I can't get him to admit it, but I'm certain he was mixed up in Jonas's crash. Aren't you?"

Hunter didn't react right away. He thought hard. "Matt Fortune is a pretty extreme guy," he said, more to himself than to me. "Difficult to like. But that doesn't make him a killer."

"So why does Zoey get nightmares about him?" I asked. "Why does he blow a fuse when I put pressure on him?"

Hunter frowned. "That's the risk I'm taking—that you're right on this, that Matt was involved."

If my resolve was going to break, this was the moment. I felt Hunter's gaze drill through me, looking for that weak spot.

"If you're wrong, we waste Jonas's last chance."

I swallowed hard. "I'm not wrong."

"Then this is the plan," Hunter explained.

"What we need is to create a replica of the crash situation."

Once Hunter had shared his plan with me, we waited for Phoenix and Arizona to come back from Amos Peak. Then he called for Jonas, Summer, Iceman, Eve, and Donna to join us in a "vital meeting"—his words.

The moment Phoenix walked into the house, I'd felt a rush of warmth, as if the sun had come out after months of rain. I bathed in his presence, my spirit at ease. Him too: his face lit up when he saw me.

"We need Matt there, riding the highway on his Harley as close to Turkey Shoot Ridge as we can get him," Hunter said.

"That's easy," Arizona agreed. "We wait for him to lead the memorial procession on Tuesday."

"Exactly twelve months after the event," Summer added. She stood close to Jonas as if to support him. "So we're cutting it pretty fine."

"And what does Darina have to do between now and then?" Phoenix wanted to know.

"Lie low," Hunter assured him. "Don't worry, she won't put herself into any more danger before Tuesday."

Phoenix held my hand. His was big and broad. Mine was small, nestling inside his, our fingers laced together. "Then what?" he asked.

"Then she plays a catalyst role." Hunter's voice didn't shift from the calm, authoritative note he always used. "Darina already knows what she has to do."

"I'll be part of the procession," I told Phoenix. "Either following in my car or riding on one of the bikes—I'm not sure yet. We'll all drive slowly out of town. When we reach the place by the neon cross, where the back road branches off, I'll come alongside Matt and challenge him."

I felt Phoenix grip my hand tighter. "Challenge him?" he echoed. I could feel him trying to control his anxiety.

"I say something to him that will make him flip. Something linked with Jonas's crash. I throw him so far off balance that he leaves the procession and chases me."

"No way!" Phoenix protested. He stepped right up to Hunter. "I won't let you do that—it's way too dangerous."

Arizona took half a step forward to tell him to back off. Summer put her hand to her mouth. Jonas and the others looked stunned.

Hunter tilted his head back, gathered himself, then silenced Phoenix by zapping his strength so that his legs buckled and he sank to the floor. "Any other objections?" he demanded.

Phoenix dragged himself onto his knees and I ran to him. "It's OK—I've already said I'd do it. I *want* to do it—for Jonas."

"Phoenix agrees with Hunter's plan—don't you, Phoenix?" It was Arizona who put the words into his mouth and carried us all forward. "How does it go from there, Darina?"

"I lead Matt a short way up the track to where Hunter's waiting. There's the three of us—Hunter, me, and Matt." I took a deep breath before I delivered the crunch idea. "That's when we travel back in time."

"Exactly twelve months." Hunter left Phoenix helpless on the floor and fixed his gaze on Jonas. "Same time, same place."

"You take them both back Matt and Darina?" Jonas checked. "They get to time travel?"

"Seeing is believing," Hunter nodded.

"Does she know how much it hurts?" Summer interrupted. Doubtful glances flew around the room. Hunter was hitting more resistance than I'd ever seen before.

"I know. He told me," I insisted. "This is my decision. I also know that we do this alone: Hunter, Matt, and me."

When he heard this, Phoenix struggled to his feet. He

swayed from side to side, trying to stay upright. "I want to be there," he muttered through his pain.

"No, just Hunter, Matt, and me. Because it takes a huge effort to transport us back through time," I went on, holding Phoenix by both arms to steady him. "The more people he carries back with him, the more it drains his energy and the more it hurts—you know that."

"Darina's right," Summer said softly. "You do know it, Phoenix."

He bowed his head, hating to give in but seeing there was no other way.

"So, Darina, Jonas's eternal future is down to you and you alone," Arizona said with her usual edge. "Wowee-zowee, Jonas, that sure makes a person stop and think!"

I spent the afternoon with the Beautiful Dead.

I say that without thinking twice about it, like it was normal. Like I'd done it all my life.

The sky had cleared and was an intense blue. The storm had passed us by. Or maybe my weather prayer really had worked.

Something bigger than a kite—an eagle maybe—soared over Phoenix and me as we followed Iceman to a hidden hollow beside the creek where a stack of logs was piled high, ready for winter fires.

"This is the best place to fish," Iceman told me. "From

the rock in the middle of the creek, early in the morning, just after the sun rises."

I couldn't resist stepping across stones to reach the rock, spreading my arms wide and inviting Phoenix to join me.

He shook his head. Since the argument with Hunter he'd been quiet, even distant—an emotional separation that was driving me crazy.

"It's wonderful!" I cried, standing in the sun with the clear water whirling and bubbling around me. "Hey, I can see fish!"

Brown shadows underwater—round, unblinking eyes, fat, speckled bodies, and quick, flicking tails. I lay down on the rock for a better view.

When I looked up, Phoenix was with me and Iceman had disappeared.

"Why is Iceman called Iceman?" I asked with a bright smile that said *You came across to be near me!*

"He climbed mountains," Phoenix told me. "Fourteeners—way above the snow line."

"With crampons and ice axes and all that stuff?" Climbing a fourteen thousand-foot mountain in the snow wasn't my thing, though I knew people who did it.

Phoenix nodded. "One day his rope broke and he fell. They never found his body. That's why he's here with us."

I shivered and moved in closer. "Let's talk about sunshine

sparkling on the water, fat fish waiting to be caught. You and me."

"Let's not talk," he said, kissing me instead.

Warmth, light, and love. Before Tuesday. Before I took the giant step back through time for Jonas.

10

On the scale of stuff that makes me nervous, this scored way higher than anything else I'd ever done. I could probably sky dive for a nine out of ten, take a flight in a spaceship for ten. But this—traveling back in time—was eleven for sure.

Tuesday after school. Jonas Day.

"Darina, you look awful," Laura told me when I went to see her in the store after I drove back from Foxton. "Has something bad happened?"

I shook my head. I'd spent my paradise time with Phoenix by the creek, like ordinary lovers—sharing, smiling, holding, touching, not needing to talk. Wishing we *were* ordinary, not this crazy mix of real and unreal, human and half human.

"This is how it would have been," I'd sighed, nestling against him. *If you hadn't got yourself killed.*

"This *is* how it is," he'd replied.

Then we'd done our sweet sorrow parting thing without the sweetness.

"I have to walk you to your car now." Phoenix had stood up from the bank and offered me his hand.

"Says who?" I'd looked around and there'd been no one there.

"Hunter," Phoenix had replied.

"Hunter!" I'd said in the same instant. The overlord.

Phoenix pushed out his bottom lip and grimaced. "He says it's time to say good-bye."

I'd stood up slowly. "Until when?"

"Until after Tuesday, when it's over." He'd led the way along the creek, occasionally glancing over his shoulder to check that I was following.

Again I'd felt a distance between us. I'd run to catch up. "Does that mean I can't come here before then?"

Phoenix had stopped by a tall, smooth boulder whose granite surface sparkled with flecks of white. He'd leaned back against it, hands in his pockets, looking up at the sky. "Here's the deal—from the way Summer explains it, we need to rest up. Every time, before something big happens, we keep a low profile, hoping that we don't have to use too much energy, just concentrating and building up to what we have to do."

"So time travel is big, even for the Beautiful Dead?" I'd quizzed, my stomach flipping and churning like the fish in the creek.

"Next to the first journey from limbo back here to the far side, it's the biggest," he'd admitted. "It takes a whole lot of power—that's why Hunter only uses it after he's tried everything else, a kind of end game."

Deep breaths. *Keep calm.* I'd put on my brave smile for him. "What about you? Do you think that's really where we're at?"

Phoenix hadn't replied. Instead, he'd put his arms around me and held me tighter than he meant to, his lips against the top of my head, rocking me gently back and forth.

"You didn't crash your new car?" Laura asked me now, to account for how pale and shaky I looked.

I clicked my tongue against my teeth.

"You had a fight with Jim?" she guessed.

"No, honestly, Mom, I'm good." I'd driven down from Foxton and drifted aimlessly into the store. Now I was beginning to wish I hadn't. Besides putting myself under Laura's Spanish Inquisition, I'd spotted a gang of kids from school pulling up in the parking lot, including Lucas, Jordan, and Matt. I dodged into a nearby changing cubicle to make sure they didn't see me.

Laura didn't let up. "Since when did you fight with Jordan?" she wanted to know, nosily peering through the window and jumping to the wrong conclusion. "I thought you two were close."

"We are. It's not her, it's Matt." And, with a neat, swift piece of topic-changing footwork that I was getting so good at, I let Laura into some of my reasons for keeping my distance from Matt Fortune. "He always made trouble between me and Zoey. Plus, he's an asshole."

"Darina!" Laura glanced around to see if any customers had overheard.

"He is. He made a fool of himself the other day, shouting and turning nasty when I said something he didn't like."

Laura's jaw dropped. "What do you mean, he turned nasty? Was he mean? Did he fight with you?"

I nodded. "He just acted like a crazy person. Everyone was staring. Luckily, Brandon was there."

Stung once, twice, three times. One, Matt was violent. Two, he publicly humiliated me. Three, Brandon Rohr was involved. Laura reeled from the shock. "When was this exactly? Where's my phone? I need to call Jim."

Feeling smug for distracting Laura, I made my way out of the store—only to bump into Logan, who was hanging out in the mall with Christian.

There was an awkward silence between Logan and me until Christian filled it with stuff about my new car and his next fight in the Senior High Middleweight League, coming up next Thursday in North Carolina.

"That's two days after Jonas's memorial deal," Christian reminded me, as if I needed it. "My trainer gave me the time off to be there."

"Along with the whole of Ellerton High." Logan said he'd run into one of the school professors, who'd told him the teaching staff planned to attend—even Dr. Valenti. "Everyone loved Jonas," he added. "We all miss him."

I could have picked that up and run with it. *You mean, not everyone loved Phoenix. Not everyone misses him?* But I didn't have the energy. So I smiled at Christian, wished him luck with his training, and walked on, making the excuse that I had to pick up a message on my phone. Which was true.

The text was from Zoey and it read, Mom driving me 2 mall. Meet at Starlite in 5.

I was stunned. I felt as if I'd already done the time jump and the Zoey in the message was the one I'd known before the crash. Zoey was coming to the mall on a Saturday afternoon. She wanted to meet up in the same old place.

I texted her back, C u there, and ran across the parking lot in time to see Mrs. Bishop lifting her daughter's high-tech wheelchair out of the trunk then standing back to let Zoey step out of the car unaided.

"Ta-dah!" Zoey glanced up and saw me standing there with my jaw hanging open. "Watch me!"

She took one step, two, then three. Her mom stood ready to dive forward to save her. I shook my head, amazed.

Three steps and she reached the chair. Slowly she turned and sat in it. She looked up at me and smiled.

I was crying, I was laughing, I was hugging her, then remembering Mrs. Bishop and trying to say hi and how cool this was, and I couldn't believe it and I was so proud of Zoey, and still I couldn't believe it!

Zoey's mom was welling up too. She took my hand and squeezed it. "We have an appointment with the hairdresser, and Zoey wants to buy new clothes."

"My old ones are so not cool," Zoey said. "Mom, why don't you run along to the hairdresser and leave me here in the diner with Darina?"

"Are you sure?" Mrs. Bishop hesitated, but not for long. Like me, she thought she'd got her old Zoey back. "Yes, great idea—give you two time to catch up."

And she went, stretching to a breaking point the invisible cord that attached her to the sick Zoey, constantly glancing over her shoulder as she walked on down the sidewalk to her hairdresser.

"Look at you!" I sighed to Zoey, following her whizzy wheelchair into Starlite's, ignoring the fact that she was way too pale, way too thin, and her smile was only skin deep.

The waitress moved a chair to make space at a table. A few people stared.

"Yeah, look at me," Zoey sighed. Once she let go of the surface smile, I could see the pain in her eyes. "Truth, Darina. How much will hair color and a makeover do for me?"

"It's a start," I said, letting my own smile grow sadder. "And the walking thing, Zoey—it's amazing."

"I promised Kim." Zoey stared straight at me, refusing to take notice of the other customers. "I said I'd come to town at least once before my next therapy session."

"And you did."

"I'm here," she agreed, but flatly. "And dying every step of the way."

"It'll get easier."

"You think?"

The waitress brought our Cokes with the smile that you put on for people who have been unlucky in life. "Something to eat?" she asked.

Zoey shook her head. "I did it—I made Mom drive me in. But I'm a wuss. I had to text you to get me through this."

"I'm glad you did." Desperate not to patronize, I said almost nothing. I hoped my eyes were saying it all for me.

And it was going well. Zoey grew more relaxed, sharing with me that her physical therapist had given her new routines to work on, when Matt Fortune, Lucas, and Jordan walked in.

God give him the decency not to walk up to us! I prayed. Literally—I prayed. God didn't hear me. For a split second, Matt looked thrown off balance then he crossed toward us. "Hey, Zoey, how are you doing?" he said, straddling a chair at our table while Lucas and Jordan hung back.

"Good, thanks." Zoey whispered without seeming to move her lips. She attempted a smile for the other two but it didn't happen.

"I'm shocked," Matt went on. "Don't get me wrong, Zoey, you look cool, but I didn't expect to see you here."

I wondered if he was hassling us just so that he could get back at me. It was a Matt Fortune type of action. Or maybe he had an even worse, deeper reason, directly to do with Zoey.

"Hey, guys, come and say hi!" he called to Lucas and Jordan. "I was telling Zoey, we didn't expect her to be back so soon."

As they came across I kept my eyes on Zoey, saw that she was trembling, and snuck her a look that asked if she wanted to get out of there. She gave me the smallest possible nod.

"Hi, Jordan, Lucas. Sorry we have to go meet Mrs. Bishop at the hairdresser's," I said, hurriedly pushing back my chair, flinching at the scraping noise. I made room for Zoey to exit.

"Well, Zo, you're doing great." Matt too made a big deal of making space. "So maybe, since you're feeling better, you'll be there Tuesday."

I wanted the ground to open and swallow us. I looked straight into Matt Fortune's weird flecked eyes and I wanted to kill him.

"Tuesday?" Zoey repeated in the smallest whisper. She obviously didn't know a thing about it.

"Jonas's memorial procession," he explained. "It's one year to the day. But then, I don't need to tell you that."

Zoey went straight back to her car. "Open the door," she begged. "Darina, please open it."

"I don't have the key!" I was feeling sick to my stomach, desperately looking around for Mrs. Bishop. Matt was still in the diner with Lucas, while Jordan was running down the sidewalk, presumably to fetch Zoey's mom.

Zoey sagged forward in her chair. "Why didn't anyone tell me? Darina, how long have you known about this memorial thing?"

"Not long. Matt's planned it. Everyone else just fell in behind him."

"Why? It doesn't make sense."

"To honor Jonas—that's the reason he gives. From anyone else it would be cool." I crouched next to Zoey, gripping the arm of her chair.

"But not from Matt," she breathed, shaking with sobs. "Matt didn't like Jonas. He hated him."

"Exactly."

"When I see his face in my nightmares, that's what it's filled with—hate. It's in his eyes, the way his mouth twists in a fake smile. That's what I can't bear."

"Me neither." All I could do was hold her hand.

"What is it with him? Why can't he leave me alone?"

"I think he's scared," I said quietly—the first time I'd voiced it, even to myself. "Beneath the hate, he's scared of what you know."

Zoey looked up. For a millisecond I thought she'd remembered but then it faded. "Darina, you know how it feels when your heart breaks—the exact moment it happens?"

I nodded.

Her eyes were tragic and swollen; her mouth had lost its shape. She'd slipped beyond help. "I lost Jonas, and crack, my heart split in two. Like you with Phoenix."

I put my hand over my mouth, but the sob escaped between my fingers in a warm rush.

"And you know the worst thing—the very worst?" Zoey waited for me to answer, knowing that I knew.

"You never got to say good-bye," I whispered.

Mrs. Bishop came running and got Zoey into the car. "I trusted you to take care of her," she told me bitterly.

I watched the car drive out of the mall. Then I walked away from Jordan who was admitting that Matt was wrong to blurt it out that way, he had no people skills, and that's how guys were.

"He didn't plan to do this to Zoey," she called after me.

"You have no idea what Matt planned," I yelled back.

My heart was racing; I was overcome with sorrow. "Zoey did *not* need to know that!" I repeated out loud as I got behind the wheel and drove out of the lot. "Especially not from Matt Fortune." The news had blown apart her shaky path toward a future without Jonas, like a landmine exploding beneath her feet. And he'd delivered it without caring what it would do to her, thinking only about himself. *I am the leader of the grief procession. I wear leathers and ride Harleys. Everyone, follow me.*

Zoey had almost died in that crash. She'd lost Jonas.

I drove fast out of town into the gathering dusk, reaching Turkey Shoot Ridge and turning left onto the back road just as the blue light of the neon cross began to glow.

As always, the force field on Foxton Ridge hit me hard. I was out of the car and heading for Angel Rock. The mountains were black against a purple sky and a million wings battered me, took my breath, bruised my racing heart. I didn't care. I could fight through it, knowing what lay on the other side. *It's me, Darina. I know I'm not supposed to be here, but let me through!*

But the wings were strong, like a storm over my head, driving me back. I lost my footing and slid down a granite slope, landing in bushes, feeling thorns catch and tear at my skin as I crawled out. Then I sat with my hands around my knees, curled up on the mountainside, waiting for it to ease. Endless millions of lost souls, a storm of thrashing wings pressed down on me, and I cried for them in their desperate sorrow.

Through my tears I saw the death heads—many skulls surrounding me, appearing out of the shadows, swooping toward me as if their sightless eye sockets had the power to see—dark holes in the skulls above rows of grinning teeth. They came closer, closer, drawing me into the nothingness behind their eyes.

"Hunter!" I cried out to the overlord of the Beautiful Dead. I was almost sucked in, on the point of losing any grip on why I'd come and who I'd come to see. I shouted the one name that remained inside my head.

A tall figure appeared by Angel Rock. It strode toward me in a weird half-light, almost glowing like the cross on the hill.

"Hunter," I gasped. "Make them stop."

He strode through the storm of pounding wings, his long hair blown back as he crossed the smooth rock where I'd slipped and fallen. When he reached me and stretched out his hand, the death heads had gone.

"Stand up," he said. As soon as I was on my feet he let go of my hand and gazed icily into my eyes, reading my reason for being there. Slowly he shook his head.

"Let me explain," I begged. I gathered the scraps of strength I had left to keep my own gaze steady, in spite of the wings crowding around us. "You know how much I want to help Jonas and the others—I've proved it to you. But there's Zoey too. She's hurting. You have no idea—."

"That doesn't concern me," Hunter interrupted. "You disobeyed me, Darina. Phoenix told you to stay away until we were through with Tuesday. You understand why."

"I do. But I just met with Zoey—you know that too, don't you? She was making big steps forward. Coming to the mall was a huge thing for her, it's taken her a whole year. Then Matt destroys her all over again."

"She's young. Her heart will mend." Hunter was still staring at me, searching for something I didn't understand. He didn't look angry anymore.

"It won't mend," I argued. "Not until she's said good-bye to Jonas."

It was a deal. Hunter would allow Jonas to pay Zoey a visit. He didn't let me thank him, said he wasn't doing it out of kindness—but because I was putting myself on the line for the Beautiful Dead and deserved some payback.

"When you leave here, go straight to Zoey's place," he instructed. "Jonas will come soon after."

"Thank you," I said anyway. "She'll talk with Jonas but then he'll zap her memory and she won't recall a thing. Is that how it works?"

Hunter nodded. "She'll be in pain. That's why you need to be there."

The pain—I'd forgotten about that. It made me shudder. But then I remembered that Bob Jonson and the other vigilantes had been through it and were still living and breathing. But then they were tough guys and Zoey had already been through so much...

"You thought it was simple," Hunter said with a faint smile. "But it never is."

I drove back and found Zoey in the stable yard with her two horses. The yard was brightly lit by lights with sensors that responded to movement. She was in her wheelchair, close to Pepper's door.

"Go find her," Mrs. Bishop had told me when I'd rung the

doorbell. "I'm sorry I yelled at you earlier, Darina. Zoey told me about Matt and the memorial procession. She's so trauma-tized; I can't begin to tell you. It's…well, it's affecting me."

I'd told her that she had no reason to apologize. "It brings the whole thing back. The crash, losing Jonas—everything."

"Her father's gone to visit Dr. Valenti. He says the cere-mony is inappropriate—the Harleys and all. He wants the school to stop it if it can."

If I hadn't made my pact with the Beautiful Dead, this would have been music to my ears. As things stood, my heart had almost stopped beating. So I'd gone ahead, through the hall into Zoey's room and out through the patio doors into the stable yard. And she'd glanced at me and turned away with a shake of her head.

She didn't want anyone in her world except the one person she couldn't have.

I waited.

The sound of the wings began softly, enough to alert Merlin and Pepper, but not to startle them. They stretched their heads out over the stable doors. Zoey paid no atten-tion. In a dark corner of the yard a shimmering shape appeared. The security light didn't respond.

The shape was pale at first, glowing yellow and red around the edges and creating an effect like light seeping into the edge of a reel of celluloid film. Then Zoey sensed that someone was there. She looked with wide, shining eyes toward the emerging figure.

Jonas appeared. He didn't move or say a word until she recognized him. Then he smiled.

Zoey's eyes opened wider still and she leaned forward in her chair. She checked and double-checked that Jonas was really there.

"Hey," he breathed, taking a step toward her. There was everything in his expression: shock at how sick she looked, sorrow at having lost her, but most of all—undiluted love.

"Jonas." She breathed his name, gripping the arms of her chair and slowly raising herself until she stood unsteadily by Pepper's door. Her face was transformed. This was a miracle happening in front of her eyes. "You came back."

Jonas ran toward her and scooped her up. She flung her arms around his neck, sobbing and laughing at the same time. She buried her head against his shoulder while he held her close.

"Put me down—I'm too heavy," she said after the longest embrace.

"You're light as a feather," he smiled, putting her back on her feet and stroking her hair. "You need to eat."

Zoey put her fingertips to his lips. Then she spotted the tiny angel-wing tattoo on his neck. "This is new."

He nodded. There was too much to explain—stuff that she was never going to remember, so he just held her.

"You left me all alone," she whispered, her lips against his cheek. "Where did you go?"

It was agony for him. All he wanted to do was kiss her and keep her silent.

"I crashed the Dyna," he reminded her. "I'm so sorry. I loved you more than my life."

"Say that you love me now," she pleaded. "That you won't leave me again."

"I *do* love you more than anything. I'll never love anyone else."

"I love you too," she echoed.

"Remember Hartmann Lake?"

"The cool water. You, holding my hand."

"One of your shoes slipped into the water."

"You fished it out." Zoey smiled with trembling lips. She held every diamond detail inside her head—how the reeds had parted and the shoe had floated like a canoe. "And now I'm holding you, I can see your blue eyes, feel your soft lips."

"Eat!" he pleaded with her. "Don't fade away."

"I will."

"Promise me."

"I promise."

"Learn to walk again."

"Watch me!" she whispered, loosening her hold of Jonas just long enough to take two steps away from him and two steps back. She smiled at him as if she'd walked a tightrope across the Grand Canyon.

"Be strong." Jonas held her tight again. Over her shoulder he saw me standing quietly in the far corner of the yard. "Even when you don't see me anymore or hear my voice, be strong."

For a long time Zoey didn't seem to move. But her hold on Jonas was slowly slackening, until she stood upright and stared at him. "You're going away again?"

"I need to—I don't have any choice. I love you, Zoey."

"You won't come back?"

"I love you." There was nothing else he could say. Nothing he could do.

Zoey's lips moved to say the same three words, so quiet that even Jonas didn't hear. Then she whispered, "Good-bye."

Jonas left the yard the way the Beautiful Dead do—there one second as solid and alive as can be, then shimmering and fading away to nothing.

Zoey closed her eyes and I helped her back into her chair, holding her hand as her body turned cold and started to shake as if she'd been dragged half dead from a frozen lake. Her face was deathly white.

"It'll be OK," I murmured.

Her head fell back against the chair, exposing her long neck, thin and delicate as a bird's. Her eyes rolled under lids threaded with deep blue veins.

"Hold on," I pleaded, scared to death by her shallow breathing. "It'll soon be over."

Zoey arched her back and clung to my hand, still trembling but starting to make her eyes focus on her surroundings. She turned her head toward me and spoke my name. "Darina?"

I nodded and breathed deeply. "Hold on," I whispered.

"I can hear wings," she said in a tiny voice. "They're all around. And my head hurts. Where am I? What just happened?"

I was sworn not to explain, so I waited in silence.

"Unbelievable. I never heard so many wings—a great flock of birds—but I didn't see them." Zoey sighed and licked her dry lips. "I saw Jonas."

I waited again.

"In a dream. No, it was more than an ordinary dream, it was a vision. Jonas, just as he used to be."

I watched anxiously, stroking her arm.

"We were so happy. Unbelievably happy. Then we said good-bye. And now I feel totally different—not heavy anymore. I can't describe it."

"No need," I told her.

"I don't feel afraid," she confided. "I know Jonas has

gone away and he won't come back. And I felt pain, but somehow I'm not alone anymore." Color was returning to her face, she was breathing evenly.

My face was wet with tears of gladness.

"I don't hear the wings. They've stopped." Zoey looked around the yard as if slowly waking from anesthesia. "That was so amazing!"

"I'm so happy for you." Use any words—a weight lifting, shackles falling away, sun coming out from behind the clouds—that was what had happened to Zoey. Jonas had broken his promise to make her forget. But then, how could he have not? Phoenix would have done the same thing. And in that moment, I knew that Hunter must have known, as well.

"I have my life back," she breathed.

I slipped my hand into my jeans pocket and slowly drew out Jonas's silver buckle. Always Stay True to the Core. I handed it to her.

She let it lie in the palm of her hand. Then, with a look of wonder, she raised it to her lips and kissed it.

11

Then there was the normal, everyday stuff to get through.
Laura told Jim how Matt had gone crazy on me, and
Jim went to see Charlie Fortune—the only family Matt
had in Ellerton. He came back with Charlie's promise that
Matt would back off from now on.

I loaded my thanks with sarcasm. A. Because I can take
care of myself, and B. Because Jim's ploy wouldn't work.
In fact, it was guaranteed to make Matt even meaner
than before.

On Sunday word got around that Mr. Bishop had called
on Dr. Valenti to try and stop Tuesday's procession, but it
turned out the principal had no powers beyond the school
gates. "What the students do in their own time is down to
them," was the message. And he'd suggested that Zoey's dad
should talk to the sheriff, to check on the traffic situation
to see if Matt's motorcade was breaking any laws. Which
shows the limits of Il Duce's imagination, but it didn't help
the Bishops.

Oh, and then there was Logan.

He came to my place late on Sunday afternoon, minus either the aggressive come-ons or the negative signals he'd been giving off lately and more like the old, chilled Logan. We sat out on the porch like we'd done a million times before.

"Aren't you going to ask me if I did my homework?" I kidded. "Or if I checked the oil gauge in my car?"

"Yeah, I'm a pain in the ass." He sighed, stretching out his legs and sitting back on the creaky swing. "I'm hard to live with, huh?"

"We've had a few crossed wires lately," I agreed, happy that he was keeping his distance. Then again, I wasn't exactly come-on material. I'd slept late and stayed indoors, trying to recover from the day before. So I wasn't wearing mascara, and I was slopping around in old jeans and a T-shirt.

Logan swung and creaked for a while.

"And you're definitely not going to tell me you'll wait for me until I'm ready to fall in love with you," I heard myself challenge. *Let's get this clear, Logan, once and for all.*

He stopped the swing and stared at me. "You sure don't care about hurting my feelings, do you?"

"That's stupid, and you know it." *Truth time.* "No way do I want to hurt you, but you've got to stop crowding me the way you've been doing lately. It's not like that between us—we're friends. At least, I hope we are."

"Friends." He nodded, managing to convey in one word a world of disappointment and disillusionment.

"Hey, don't trash it. I don't have very many. You're one of the lucky few. Or unlucky, depending on how you look at it…"

"Meaning, you'll come to me with a problem if you have one?"

"Sometimes, yes."

"Not always?"

"No. Some things are private. I like it that way."

"And I can still talk to you about stuff?"

"Whenever." The literal way Logan needed to fix boundaries made me smile. "So what's up?"

Logan started with the swing again. "Am I that easy to read?"

"Like an open book."

"OK, I just had to get away from my house because Bob Jonson is back drinking with Dad. I don't like to see it."

I cringed. "No, it's not good."

"He needs to clean up before Tuesday, and I'm not sure he can—not if Dad comes across with the alcohol and lets him drink himself stupid."

Something struck me about Logan then that I should've paid attention to before, only you don't when you're around someone so much. Logan was the parent and his dad was the child—totally the wrong way around. And now he had Bob Jonson to deal with as well. "It's not up to you," I said quietly.

"And it's not just the Buds and the whiskey chasers," Logan went on. "We all know what's coming up—the anniversary and all—which is hard enough for Bob without the big procession thing. Tuesday might push him over the edge."

I sat forward in my chair. "I thought you backed Matt on that. I thought everyone did."

"I'm not so sure, Darina. I'd be happier if someone else was heading it. This way, it feels…dangerous. Kind of, light the fuse and stand back. Does that sound stupid?"

He had my attention now, every particle of it. "No. Explain."

"Matt's an out of control type of guy. And he never organized anything like this before. There'll be a lot of bikes—a hundred maybe. And emotions are running high. But Valenti sanctioned it—did you hear?"

"What he actually said was he couldn't stop it." I agreed with everything Logan said, but I still desperately needed Jonas's memorial procession to go ahead.

"Yeah, so there's nothing I can do," Logan agreed. "Except be there on one of Charlie's bikes."

"We all have to be there," I insisted. And right there on the spot, I made up my mind about where I wanted to be, too, come Tuesday. "Can I ride with you?" I asked. "Up near the front, alongside Bob and Matt?"

Normal, everyday stuff. School on Monday, chatting with Jordan and Hannah, hearing Matt endlessly using his phone, pinning down details of time and place, speaking to his brother about the number of bikes on loan.

In the afternoon he cornered me. "Hey, daddy's girl!"

We were between classes, on a stairway with a long-distance view of Amos Peak. There was no one else around.

"Back off, Matt," I warned him.

"Aw, does daddy's little girl need protecting from big bad Matt?"

He knew Jim wasn't my dad; he was just twisting the knife. I tried to dodge free, but he pushed me back against the stair rail.

"You know what I told Jim when he came visiting? I told him he must be kidding. No way would I waste my time hassling his stepdaughter, Little Miss Weirdo. She's not my type, I said. Anyway, I asked him: Did you take a good look at her lately? Since Phoenix died, she really let herself go."

My head was reeling and I felt nauseous. Half of me wanted to punch him. The other half wanted to crawl into a hole and die.

"Hey, Matt, did Charlie find me a bike yet?" Christian called up from the bottom of the stairwell.

That seemed to break the spell. Matt gave me one last sneer and ran down to join him, two steps at a time.

School on Tuesday and I hadn't slept all night. The school parking lot was filled with gleaming chrome. A spontaneous contest grew up between the girls over who had bought the biggest and best red roses, the flower of love. They stacked them on the steps outside the main door, ready to carry in the procession.

At midday I had a message from Zoey: Am wearing J's buckle and thinking of u all.

At lunch Logan sat next to me and we didn't talk.

I didn't connect with anything—not the Harleys or the roses, or the fact that clouds were gathering over the mountains. All I knew was that this was end game for Jonas and I'd better not screw up.

"There's a fifty percent chance of a storm before sundown," Logan told me as I climbed on the back of his borrowed Softail bike. We followed a stream of Harleys, Kawasakis, and Suzukis out of the school grounds toward the center of town.

"Crap," I muttered.

"Why so jittery?" Logan could feel me trembling as I put my arms around his waist. "You're not freaking out over me riding this thing, are you?"

"No, Logan. I'd trust you with my life," I muttered as he handed me a helmet. I strapped it on.

We coasted along at twenty miles per hour, in the center of a bunch of other riders, part of a big pack.

Logan glanced over his shoulder, looking out for Matt. "He said Charlie, Brandon, and some of the older guys will meet us at the mall. About twenty in all. Plus thirty-five of us from Ellerton High. Plus who knows how many kids in cars."

"Here comes Matt now." I'd spotted him riding up from the rear, sitting well back on his seat, arms outstretched and the fringes on his leather jacket fluttering in the wind as he wove through the pack.

He yelled instructions above the roar of the bikes. "Here's the order of riders in the procession. Tommy, you ride with Lucas. Logan and Christian, you're behind them. Don't tailgate, and don't overtake."

We stopped at red lights and Logan had time to turn around properly. "You OK?" he asked me. "Are you sure you want to do this?"

"I'm hating every second, but yes, I want to be here."

The lights changed and we crossed the highway to ride into the mall with big, slow drops of rain starting to fall.

Matt rode ahead, right up to his brother, who was sitting astride his Tourer, waiting with his own bunch of friends for the event to start.

Logan and I coasted around the edge of the parking lot, looking to take up position behind Tommy and Lucas, who had Jordan riding with him. "These guys are hardcore," she muttered over the idling engines.

Among Brandon's group of friends there were no shiny jackets with fringes, no clean blue jeans. Instead, their leathers were creased and scuffed, covered in studs and zippers. Some had long hair and beards and looked like they were joined at the hip to their pennant-flying Harleys. Very few of them wore helmets.

Brandon caught sight of me on Logan's bike and quickly looked away. Like he hadn't saved me from drowning or given me a new car. Like he didn't even know me.

"I don't see Bob Jonson," I told Logan, shaking off the weird feeling of Brandon's ignoring me. "Maybe he didn't make it."

"No surprise there." He edged through the stationary bikes to pull up alongside Christian. "The last time I saw Bob was late Sunday, smashed out of his skull."

"Again, no surprise," Christian chipped in. "The guy hasn't been sober in a month. They say now that Jonas's mom has left home for good."

Still clinging to Logan, I shook my head. "I sure hope Bob doesn't show today."

I knew it wasn't the place to spend the first anniversary of your son's death, even if you were sane, happily married, and sober. The thrum of fifty bike engines sounded their steady, background roar, waiting riders revved and stared ahead without talking. Meanwhile, the rain fell more heavily. Any heavier, and riding would become very dangerous—not to mention what a thunderstorm would do to the Beautiful Dead.

"He has less than five minutes to get here," Logan checked his watch then took a long look at the crowd that had gathered in the entrance to the mall. He noticed faces near the front and tapped my leg. "Zoey's here with her mom."

It was like someone had taken a swipe at my legs with a baseball bat and knocked my feet from under me, I was so shocked. "This isn't supposed to happen," I spluttered, jumping off the bike without thinking and running to talk with Zoey. She was standing—though leaning on her mom for support—and stunning: in a long, stylish dress with a wide belt, and Jonas's buckle. "What are you doing here?" I whispered. "I wanted to be here after all," she told me, with a smile that told me I needn't have worried. "I don't want to follow the procession. I just need to see it leave."

"There are so many people here," Mrs. Bishop said sadly.

"Everyone loved him," Zoey said, her voice as calm as I'd heard in over a year. She handed me a single red rose and told me to fix it to my lapel. "This is for Jonas. Lay it in the place where it happened. From me."

Matt was talking to Charlie and Brandon, checking watches and wondering what to do when Bob Jonson finally showed up.

He was riding his Dyna—no swerving or swaying—straight toward them, his head bare, his chin clean shaven, wearing a white T-shirt and no jacket in spite of the rain. He almost could have been mistaken for Jonas himself.

"The poor guy made it after all," Jordan murmured. "He got it together for the anniversary."

Bob rode up alongside Matt without saying a word. He looked straight ahead. "Let's go." Matt raised his right hand and pointed to the mountains.

Engines roared; pennants fluttered; the gleaming procession had started. We rolled out of town at not much more than walking pace, allowing time for the cars to fall in behind the bikes and for bystanders to realize what was going on and to pay their respects.

It must have been something to look at—the bikes, the kids, the red flowers in the rain. I spotted Laura at the door of her store, and a little later, Dr. Valenti with some of the teachers, gathered by the gas station. But most of the faces were a blur.

Soon we reached the neat lawns and picket fences of Centennial. Another blur. I was looking only at Matt Fortune, riding out there in front, judging our speed and working out how long it would take for us to reach Turkey Shoot Ridge. Then we were on the highway, rising up into the mountains under dark, threatening skies.

I leaned forward, as close to Logan as I could get.

"Whatever happens here, I want to thank you ahead of time," I told him.

He tensed up. "Why? What's going to happen?"

Ahead, Matt and Bob rode side by side, with only Lucas and Tommy between them and us. The neon cross was already plain to see.

"Something big," I whispered back. "Trust me."

We were a huge cavalcade moving along the highway, almost the only traffic on the road, toward the spot where Jonas had lost his life.

I saw Bob Jonson slow down and hang his head, his unsteady hands letting his bike wobble and swerve. I saw Matt ride close, reach out, and straighten him up. We were directly under the cross. Rain was driving into our faces.

"Logan, get up there!" I hissed.

I felt him stiffen with surprise.

"Now," I begged. "Trust me. Ride alongside Matt."

Logan gave into my plea and broke ranks. He swerved around Lucas and Jordan to catch up with Matt and Bob.

"Dude, you've got to get through this!" Matt was telling Bob.

"Don't tell me what I need to do!" Bob shouted back. He swerved away angrily, leaving space for Logan to ride between them.

Behind us, the whole procession slowed almost to a halt. We'd reached the turnoff for the back road to Angel Rock.

"You!" I yelled at Matt Fortune, leaning out toward him and burning him with my gaze. "Look at me!" Bob jerked his head up to look at me too. I had their attention.

"This is all because of you." I was calm as I slid from the seat and ran alongside Jonas's murderer. "You killed him, Matt. A year ago today. And now you're going to pay."

I had no clear view of Matt's face as he swung his Harley toward me and tried to run me down. I was ready for him though—dodging and running toward the dirt track, drawing him away from the pack. Other bikes slowed him down as I sprinted on.

Follow me, you jerk, I silently commanded Matt, listening for the sound of his bike, looking out for Hunter up ahead. *Go crazy! Follow me and try to kill me too!*

Sure enough, Matt reacted with wild fury. His engine

was roaring behind me, kicking up dirt, I was out of breath and about to fling myself sideways out of his path, when Hunter stepped out from behind a rock. He stood right in front of Matt's bike, strong as an oak tree, eyes fixed on his face, zapping him and willing him to stop.

I watched Matt's willpower crumble in an instant. He let go of the handlebars and fell with the Harley on top of him, motionless, with only the wheels spinning, until Hunter lifted the bike and dragged him to his feet.

Rain pelted down, whipped by the wind, and I heard wings, louder than ever before, if that was possible, and I too was under Hunter's spell, unable to move as he grasped Matt's shoulders.

Something extraordinary was happening.

Wings were beating, a storm brewing, gray clouds cloaking the mountainside, and Matt Fortune was standing beside Hunter with wings—a devil-angel. Then I was in Hunter's grasp, surrounded by mist and feeling my shoulder blades tingle and burn. I turned around and gasped to see my own magical white wings spreading, to see that I was becoming part of that world—the world of the Beautiful Dead.

I beat my angel wings alongside a million lost souls. I could see Hunter up ahead with Matt, forging through gray mist. My feet had left the ground and my wings were moving...

But this wasn't like flying—more like spinning, tumbling, whirling through the sky without any sense of direction or control. I could see Matt's face, his mouth wide open in silent fury. And Hunter's mask-like face, stony cold. I tried not to scream.

The world grew darker. We were in the eye of the storm, tumbling and turning, our wings spread wide. I felt pain through my whole body—every muscle was stretched and twisted as we traveled. And wings surrounded me, carrying me on a violent current, along with the death faces, a hundred thousand—floating, haunting, spooking, spreading to infinity.

The yellow, crumbling skulls surrounded Matt. I lost sight of him but could still see Hunter leading the way toward a pinpoint of light ahead.

I had to reach that light. Death wanted me. It was tugging at my limbs, tearing at my beautiful wings, but I struggled on.

Hold on, Darina. I heard Phoenix's voice above the chaos. *You're almost there.*

He was watching over me. I pictured him on Foxton Ridge, standing alone, staring up into the storm, seeing everything.

The distant pinprick grew bigger, brighter. We were sucked toward it at what felt like the speed of light, so fast that I thought I would split apart and disintegrate into a million atoms. And now a blinding light surrounded us—an incandescent, unearthly light. We were inside it and everything went still. The wings stopped, the skulls vanished. Hunter spread his arms wide and we were there.

It was the afternoon of Jonas's crash. We were in a leafy street in Centennial. Zoey waited impatiently on the sidewalk for Jonas to arrive.

Hunter, Matt, and I took up position fifty yards down the street. When Matt opened his mouth to speak, no words came out. I did the same—nothing. We had no speech. We were mute, invisible observers.

Torment twisted Matt's features. Hunter's powers held him prisoner.

Soon we heard the sound of a bike and saw Jonas turn the corner. Jonas on his Dyna in the sunshine, relaxed and happy—easy rider.

Zoey smiled and waved. She looked cute in cutoff pants and a blue top, her blond hair carelessly tied back. She couldn't wait to hop on the bike and ride away.

They headed out of town and we followed. Zoey had her arms around Jonas's waist, the wind caught their hair and T-shirts as they cruised onto the highway. Two beautiful people in love. My heart squeezed. Jonas left town and picked up speed.

A truck headed downhill in the opposite direction.

A silver sports car overtook Jonas and Zoey on their final journey.

Then there was another bike on the road, coming from way behind but gaining fast. Matt saw himself on his Harley, his jacket zipped to the chin, opening the throttle and making his engine roar.

For a second I took my eyes off Jonas and Zoey to glance at devil-angel Matt. I saw total disbelief, total denial, total fear. Hunter held him, a helpless witness to his own crime.

Matt raced up the hill toward Turkey Shoot Ridge. He drew level with Jonas and Zoey. Jonas glanced sideways, recognized Matt, and braked.

"Is that it—your top speed?" Matt taunted. He swerved in close to the other bike, forcing Jonas into the break-down lane.

The sun bounced off the silver machines—sudden flashes of bright silver light. Zoey clung tighter still to Jonas. She yelled at Matt to quit. Jonas braked again, swerving back onto the highway, only to find Matt had looped back and was riding circles around him, laughing out loud.

"Quit that!" Zoey cried.

Matt laughed again—an ugly laugh—the one that came back to haunt her. He was in their faces, jostling Jonas off the road again, cutting across in front of him, and nudging him from behind. A terrified Zoey leaned into Jonas and hid her face against his shoulder.

"Come on, dude, make this a race!" Matt shouted at Jonas. He leaned back and raised his handlebars, riding on one wheel along the deserted road. He refused to let Jonas slow down, harrying him from behind like a coyote snapping at the heels of a young steer. Jonas swung wide into the fast lane, trying to escape, refusing to rise to the challenge of the maniac on his tail.

"Chicken!" Matt crowed his insult, his eyes wild, adrenaline buzzing through his body. "Come on, Jonas, race me!" He swerved again and knocked against Jonas's machine, sent him and Zoey shooting off course, back toward the breakdown lane. They'd reached Turkey Shoot Ridge and the dirt road to Angel Rock.

Matt was yelling and whooping as he made one more reckless charge. Jonas braked again. He skidded past the exit road, kicking up pebbles from the scrub margin, losing control and swerving wide across the lanes, scraping the metal barrier and bouncing off again, fighting to keep his bike upright as it curved back toward the scrub.

There was a moment—a stretched, endless, slow motion moment—when it looked as if Jonas and Zoey would make it. He regained his balance and slammed on his brakes. I almost breathed. But Matt charged him again, rode straight at him, and forced him sideways.

Jonas's already skidding wheels met the scrub, skidded some more, and threw him back onto the road.

And that was the end.

They were traveling at speed, just like the cops said.

Jonas's wheels went from under him. Metal crashed and scraped along the tarmac. Zoey was thrown clear, but Jonas went under the Harley and was trapped, slamming into the central barrier, breaking his neck, and dying there, on the spot.

Which left Matt Fortune circling the crash site like a slow, black vulture, his fringed jacket flapping open, surveying the wreck and beginning to understand what he'd done. He rode up to Jonas and saw that he was dead. Then Zoey, still breathing, eyes still open, slipping away. He leaned over her as she lost consciousness, his expression blank, the kind of expression only a murderer could understand. He'd won whatever game he was playing, but he had to kill to do it.

I still didn't breathe. Matt's face mesmerized and terrified me.

He watched Zoey's eyes close. He circled around her, once, twice, then, looking up and down the highway to make sure that there were no witnesses, he rode through a gap in the central barrier and headed back into town.

12

I got my voice back beside the broken bodies of Jonas and Zoey.

"You killed him," I whispered again.

Devil-angel Matt's face showed no emotion.

"That's the truth you've been hiding ever since it happened," I accused. "And now I know it too."

The back wheel of Jonas's bike spun silently in the sun.

"So?" Matt turned to me with his empty eyes. "What are you going to do? Everyone thinks you're crazy. Who will believe you?"

Hunter stepped in, fixing Matt with his powerful gaze. "The same everyone who thinks she's crazy, that's who. The whole town. Face it, Matt, your time is up."

His iron-gray eyes held Matt, who reacted like a trapped animal, twisting and writhing to escape.

"It's no use struggling," I told Matt calmly. "Hunter's power is too strong. You're guilty. You have to face it."

But Matt didn't have the courage. In his own warped, weak mind he began to wriggle out of it. "Jonas wimped out on me—that's why he crashed. The guy should have given me a race."

"You hounded him," I replied.

"I was fooling around, that's all."

"You never meant to kill him?" I gestured toward Jonas's limp body, his limbs twisted at odd angles, his head thrown back and to one side.

"Yeah, it was an accident."

I shook my head. "Then why didn't you come clean and tell everyone? Why didn't you race to a hospital? If it wasn't for you, Jonas would still be alive. He and Zoey would be together."

Lying on the warm tarmac surface, Zoey stirred. She turned her head and tried to raise her arm.

"You believed she was dead too. You relied on that."

"You keep your dirty mouth shut!" Matt's anger erupted at last. He lunged at me and managed to get one hand around my throat before Hunter zapped him and he slumped to the ground.

"Time to leave," Hunter decided. This time he held my hand as he invited the beating souls into our space and made my wings lift me from the scene of the crash. He left devil-angel Matt to trail painfully behind, through the whirling gray mist and hordes of wailing death heads, toward the distant point of light.

We were directly under the cross. Rain was driving into our faces...

Behind us, the whole procession slowed almost to a halt. We'd reached the turnoff for the back road to Angel Rock.

"You!" I yelled at Matt Fortune, leaning out toward him and burning him with my gaze. "Look at me!" Bob jerked his head up to look at me too. I had their attention.

"This is all because of you." I was calm as I slid from the seat and ran alongside Jonas's murderer. "You killed him, Matt. A year ago today. And now you're going to pay."

Matt's engine snarled. On my right-hand side, Bob Jonson heard my accusation and twitched furiously, as if someone had passed a thousand volts through his body. He gripped his handlebars and gritted his teeth. "Is that right, Matt? You killed my son?"

"He was there. He made Jonas race, forced him right off the road," I said, loud and clear. "Tell him, Matt. Tell it like it was."

"She's crazy," Matt muttered, pushing on up the hill by Turkey Shoot Ridge, into the driving rain. "You really believe that? Why would I arrange this memorial service for someone I killed?"

Way in the distance, thunder rattled. Bob's face suffered

another jolt of fury as Matt rode off. When he turned to look at me with the startling blue eyes he shared with Jonas, it was as if the months of agony, drunkenness, and despair had suddenly burned off and he was left with the gleaming nugget of truth. He flashed a brief sad smile. Then he opened the throttle and roared after Matt.

In his mirror, Matt saw Bob come after him. He picked up speed, raising a heavy spray that enveloped Bob as he drew close.

"Follow them!" I begged Logan, who hesitated, then gunned the motor. I felt the bike surge forward, heard the thunder roll, and saw a fork of lightning tear the black sky in two.

The two bikes ahead of us were still gathering speed. They reached the top of the hill and disappeared over the other side.

"Faster!" I urged Logan, aware now of two more riders riding alongside us. One was Charlie Fortune, the other Brandon Rohr. The rest of the confused procession had pulled onto the hard shoulder at the base of the hill.

I felt Logan tense up and crouch forward, determined not to get left behind in the cloud of spray raised by Brandon and Charlie's bikes. More lightning forked down, thunder cracked, and I knew Hunter and the Beautiful Dead were no longer around to back me up. They were in limbo. I was alone, speeding toward Foxton in a storm.

Our three bikes crested the hill together. We saw Matt and Bob swoop down into the next valley, Bob close on Matt's heels, both swerving wide to pass a slow truck, plowing through the white spray. Ahead of them lay the straggle of houses that lined the road at the Foxton turnoff.

Logan, Charlie, and Brandon stayed three abreast, gaining speed as we accelerated downhill. Ahead of us, I saw Bob gain on Matt and almost draw level then I gasped as Matt suddenly shot to the left, taking the turnoff at the last split second, hoping to fool Bob into forging on straight ahead.

Bob reacted fast. He braked and his back wheel almost skidded from under him as he veered left, across the track of the heavy silver truck. For a second, both bikes vanished from sight, then reappeared racing neck and neck down the rough road by the creek.

There was more thunder. Thin strands of white cloud clung to the mountain peaks, and the rain poured down mercilessly.

Logan reached the turnoff just ahead of Brandon and Charlie. He leaned way to the left, his knee almost scraping the road as he took the corner. Now we were on a dirt track, splashing through mud, with the creek to our right. Up ahead, Matt had gained some ground, leaving Bob trailing by about twenty yards. But Bob wouldn't give up, recklessly cutting corners and gaining on Matt again. The two bikes flashed past the old fishermen's cabins, on through the burned pine trees whose roots still clung miraculously to the steep rock face.

Under the lashing rain, Brandon rode through a puddle so deep that it threw him off course and sent his bike slithering from under him. I glanced back to see him sprawled by the side of the road, his bike still sliding sideways until it hit a rock. Brandon himself scrambled to his feet and stared helplessly as Logan and Charlie left him stranded.

The road rose through the pines. The creek lay thirty or forty feet below, its white water tumbling and roaring over black boulders.

Now Bob was almost level with Matt on his left-hand side. Both riders were soaked to the skin and spattered with mud, their hair clinging to their scalps, the muscles on their arms taut as they grasped the handlebars. Bob roared ahead by half a bike's length, flying over the rough surface. He swerved in close toward Matt, forcing him to the edge of the road. Matt braked and pulled back, escaping by inches the sheer drop into the creek. I got a glimpse of Bob's face—he was smiling.

I thought my heart would stop. *My God, this is payback! He's doing what Matt did to Jonas...*

And now Charlie was yelling, "Quit, Matt! Quit!" and

his voice was lost under the snarl of engines and the wind and rain.

But Matt picked up speed again as Bob slowed his bike and looped back, coming up behind Matt and "yee-hawing" like a crazy cowboy. He forced him on as the road rose higher above the creek.

Matt veered to the left, up against a sheer rock face. He swerved back to the right, with Bob so close behind that the grit from the road was spat up by Matt's tires into his face, the sharp stones piercing his skin and drawing blood. He didn't care—he moved closer, his wheel almost touching Matt's.

I heard Charlie yell again—this time for Bob to stop. I saw Bob draw level with Matt and lean into him, pushing him closer and closer to the edge, until, at the peak of the next hill, Bob's front wheel nudged Matt's. It seemed gentle, just a glancing touch, but enough.

Matt lost control. His Harley crested over the ridge and shot into the air, swerving and curving downward over the edge of the cliff in crazy slow motion—enough time for Matt to think, *This is it. This is what death is like,* before the bike slipped away from him and he fell through the air, tumbling down toward the clear green water, smashing against those black rocks and disappearing beneath the surface.

Matt and the bike hit the water at the same moment. Logan reached the spot and we jerked to a stop. We gazed down, in time to see the silver bike get sucked under, but too late to save Matt Fortune from drowning.

Bob saw it too. Astride his bike, the grim smile had vanished, and his look was dark and hollow. He raised his head to stare into the stormy sky, letting the rain soak his bloody face before he made his engine roar one last time.

The bike threw up grit and dirt. Bob sat firm as he aimed his Dyna toward the sheer drop.

He plummeted down. He fell like a stone and the water swallowed him. His bike smashed against the rocks and stayed there—a heap of twisted metal.

The next day I placed Zoey's red rose at the exact spot where Jonas had died.

I'd left behind in Ellerton a storm of shock and disbelief, plus the burden of witnessing these two latest deaths, and I was driving out of the horror into the future, on my way up to Foxton Ridge to find Phoenix and share the end of Matt's story with him. Also, to find out what had happened to Jonas.

Did I do OK? I asked silently as I placed the rose in the rustling silver grass by the roadside. I stood in the sun, under a big blue sky.

I knew I wouldn't get an answer until I reached the old house and barn, so I got back into my car and drove on, quietly humming the tune to "Always," a sad song that Summer used to sing. "Wherever you walk, I'm always by your side. Whenever you talk, I always hear your voice..."

Along the back route to Angel Rock, I remembered the terrifying journey back in time that I'd made with Hunter and Matt only twenty-four hours earlier, enjoying the clear warm air as I drove with the hood down. The sun on the granite made it sparkle.

Then I was on foot and running across the dry scrubland, my feet crunching over the surface, the leaves on the straggly thorn bushes turning crimson, orange, and gold in the autumn wind. I reached the shadow of Angel Rock and ran on without stopping.

"Be there!" I whispered to Phoenix, before I could even see the barn and the house. Maybe the storm had driven him away and he would never come back. Maybe I was still deep down afraid that the whole thing wasn't real. "Just be there!" I said, louder.

He strode up the hill to meet me, opened his arms, and watched me run toward him, broad shouldered and strong in his black T-shirt, his lovely face serious.

"Hold me," I told him, and I felt his arms close around me.

"Thank God, Darina." His lips moved against my hair,

then he tilted my face upward and he kissed my lips. He was cold and smooth and beautiful.

"Did you hear what happened?" I asked. "Jonas's dad drove Matt off the track, over the cliff into the creek. It was horrible. They both died."

Phoenix held me close, stroking his thumb across my cheekbone and down my jawline to rest in the small hollow between my collarbones. "You did more than OK," he told me. "Hunter told us how cool you were when you time traveled. He said your hunch was right all along."

"And when Bob Jonson finally learned the truth he flipped. He did the same thing to Matt as Matt had done to Jonas—he meant for him to die."

"He got his revenge," Phoenix said gently, staring into my eyes as if he wanted to judge how deep my own shock and terror had gone. "You'll be OK," he assured me. "In time you'll see that it was meant to be."

"But I didn't mean for Bob to die," I sobbed.

"What did he have left to live for?"

"He had closure. He could have moved forward."

Phoenix shook his head. "Not in this world. Everything he had was already destroyed." He took my hand and led me into the valley, where I saw that Hunter stood in the barn doorway surrounded by his Beautiful Dead.

It was weird. The sun shone on them and they looked more beautiful and alive than ever. Hunter especially—he looked younger and softer, almost happy.

"Where did Jonas go?" I asked Phoenix as we approached the barn and took in the presence of Summer, Arizona, Iceman, Donna, and Eve with her blond-haired baby.

"Come on, Hunter will tell you," he answered quietly.

"Welcome, Darina." Their overlord stepped forward. He seemed to look at me fondly, almost father to daughter. "Jonas found justice, thanks to you."

"What happened to him?" I asked with a trembling voice.

"The storm sent us far away into infinite darkness, and Jonas stayed with us in limbo, where we could only wait and pray. You were our only hope."

"You didn't let us down," Arizona spoke and surprised me with the warmth in her tone. Summer stood by, smiling at me as if she wanted to run forward and hug me.

"I felt the exact moment when Matt Fortune died," Hunter explained. "In limbo I saw a vision of a drowned face, a hand wedged between two jagged rocks, the current tearing at his body."

"And Bob Jonson?" I murmured.

"He came to join us instantly. He died the moment he hit the water. I saw the breath leave his body and I called Jonas to me. I said, 'Your killer is dead. And your father too.' Jonas understood why his father had to die. He turned and called Bob's name in the darkness. Out of the endless, unlit space of limbo, Bob Jonson appeared. Father and son embraced. Together they traveled on."

A question formed on my lips. *Where did they go?*

"Don't ask." Phoenix read my mind. "Nobody here knows. Only that they went together, hand-in-hand."

"And you succeeded in your first task," Hunter added.

"You believed," Summer murmured, coming up and offering me the hug she'd been longing to give.

"You're tougher than I thought," Arizona said.

"This is too much," I protested. "I did what I could, that's all. And I'll do it over again."

Hunter nodded and some of the old sternness crept back into his voice. "All in good time, Darina. For now you must go home and rest."

"Not right away. Please." More than anything, now that the Jonas thing was resolved, I wanted to be with Phoenix.

"Hunter...give us a little time." Phoenix kept his arm around my waist. It gave me a strong, steady feeling as the overlord looked at us and considered his next move.

"You have an hour," Hunter proclaimed.

Sixty whole minutes! I spun and flung my arms around Phoenix's neck. He lifted me off my feet.

Summer and Arizona laughed, Hunter gave his almost

smile. Then the Beautiful Dead turned and walked into the barn.

"Let's go," Phoenix said, dragging me through the pale yellow grass to the bank of the creek. He went ahead, picking his way carefully between the rocks, then leaping onto our favorite boulder.

"Bare feet!" I insisted, and took off my shoes. I dangled my feet in the cool, crystal water. "Look, I can see specks of gold in the sand."

Phoenix leaned sideways and dipped his finger in the water. He scooped up tiny grains of glittering metal and examined them on his fingertips. "Iron pyrites," he announced.

"What's that?"

"Fool's gold." He laughed.

"Oh! I like my version better."

"I *love* your version. I love everything about you."

Try embracing on a smooth boulder in the middle of a fast running stream. It's not easy, but we made it. A gentle hug, a tender kiss that lasted forever. Then we crossed the stream and walked barefoot though the grass, hand-in-hand.

"You forgot your shoes," Phoenix reminded me when we reached the top of the hill. There was no shadow from the tall water tower, only a slight stirring of wind through the golden aspens.

I shrugged then glanced back down at the house and

barn—the rusted red roofs, the weathered log walls, and the door still left to bang, open-shut, open-shut. It looked, as it had in the beginning, as if no one had disturbed the place in a hundred years.

I know the human heart is mechanical—made up of muscle chambers, valves, and tubes. I've sat through science class, seen it on medical dramas on TV, red, raw, and pumping.

So where does the feeling I had on that ridge come from, holding fiercely to Phoenix in those last moments before our hour was up?

A feeling so strong it swept me away, kissing him and feeling him so close, knowing that he meant everything in the world to me and always would?

We were part of that wild hillside. Our spirits were in the wind and the sky, the rustling leaves.

Phoenix didn't speak. His lips touched mine one last time, his embrace slackened. He left me with a look so full of longing that my heart melted and it was all I could do to stop myself from running after him.

But I heard wings beating softly—Hunter's warning. I stayed where I was, watching Phoenix go, knowing I would soon be back.

The story continues in Beautiful Dead: Arizona.
Coming soon…

I drove with the top down and the wings fluttered around my head in a feathery flurry, more a reminder than a warning now. *Do you know how many times I've driven out to Foxton lately? Yeah, I guess you do.*

I stopped at a red light and glanced sideways.

"Phoenix!" He was sitting in the seat Zoey had just vacated, waiting with his crooked smile.

"Jeez!" I cried. The light turned green and I eased the car across the junction, too slow for the guy behind me, who almost rammed my back fender. "Phoenix, don't do that!"

"So you want me to go away again?" he asked in that lazy, mumbling voice. "I can do that." He got ready to open the car door.

"No, don't! Listen, you almost gave me a heart attack. Let me turn off the road." I fumbled with the controls, finally jerking to a stop in a small parking lot outside a general grocery store.

"Hey, Darina," he said.

I put my hand out to touch him, to check he was—you know, real.

He grabbed my hand. "Long time, huh?"

"Forever," I breathed. I'd been counting the days, the hours, and minutes. But now Phoenix was here. I was having trouble finding something meaningful to say. Instead I stared down at our two hands, his big and broad, mine smaller and smoother, enjoying the feel of his thumb stroking my palm.

"Hunter made us stay away," he told me. "You know how he is."

"A control freak," I muttered.

"Yeah, I could make a zombie joke about him being heartless…"

"Don't."

"Bad taste?"

I nodded. No feelings, literally no heart—that's how it was when you came back from the dead. And a skin so pale it looks like sunlight never touched it. Phoenix's beautiful, smooth face made my own heart beat fast enough for two of us.

"I'm here now," he said softly. Then he made me move out of the driver's seat and he took my place. Without a word, he drove onto a road that led out of town so that five minutes later we'd left the houses behind and were heading down the dirt track that led to Deer Creek.

As the car bumped and jolted, I stared up at the sky. Not

a cloud in sight, no breeze. Good, no storms. Nothing to interfere with my time with Phoenix.

He parked the car by the creek, near a bunch of thick, low-growing golden willows. Again he grabbed me by the hand, this time to pull me out of the car and lead me past the willows to a rocky ledge overlooking the water. We stood side by side, arms around each other's waists, staring down.

The water was so clear you could see each pebble resting on the bed of the creek. It flowed smoothly, carrying the first leaves of fall on its eddying surface.

Then we sat on the rock to catch the last rays of the sun, Phoenix with his long legs crooked and offering me space to sit in between, resting my back against his chest. His arms encircled me.

"I missed you," I murmured. I twisted around to see his face—features that didn't quite fit the beauty stereotype, though his high forehead and cheekbones missed it just barely and those big, blue-gray eyes hit it right on target. No, it was the mouth that made him different—just that downward turn at one corner and the way his lips moved around those laid-back, drawled words.

He leaned forward to kiss me.

Again. Again. My body sighed. It was all I wanted. Nothing else mattered, lips to lips, seeing him up close and blurred through a fringe of dark lashes.

Phoenix pulled me back against a bank of long, dried grass and kissed me harder. I went headlong with the surge of love, stronger and more dangerous than the current of any mountain stream.

"What did I do to deserve this?" he asked, refusing to let me move away. "I mean you, Darina. You're the most beautiful thing I've ever seen. But you always surprise me, like I'm looking at you all over again for the first time. You always catch me off guard."

"And you the mind reader," I kidded. I felt myself falling away swiftly into the dark, lonely place and heaved myself back by switching the topic. "So tell me how come Hunter permitted you to show up at last?"

Phoenix shrugged. "He never gives reasons. The truth is, he only showed up again earlier today. I don't know where he's been hanging out since the Jonas thing."

"So where were you and the others?" I asked. Not at Foxton, I was certain.

Phoenix uneasily looked away. "Arizona took control. She said we had to leave Foxton for a while, let things get back to normal around there."

"So where did you go?" I insisted.

"A couple of places I'd never been before—I can't tell you exactly."

I clucked my tongue. "You mean 'won't.' As in, it's another of Hunter's rules."

"All I know is Hunter went off and Arizona took care of us and warned us not to ask any questions."

I sighed. "OK, you don't need to answer, but let me take an educated guess. Hunter went back to limbo to update whoever or whatever it is he answers to—like, an overlord-overlord. He left the Beautiful Dead in some secret hiding place, kind of hibernating until he made it back to the far side." I studied Phoenix's face for a reaction but didn't find one, which meant I was right. "That's interesting. There's someone or something telling Hunter what to do. And listen, Phoenix, I don't want to hear you telling me not to worry about it, OK?"

"As if that would do any good." He leaned back and rested his hands behind his head.

"So what was it like, taking orders from Arizona?" There was an edge to this question, I admit.

"Arizona's cool. She's real smart."

"Should I be jealous?" I only half kidded. After all, I knew dozens of boys at Ellerton High who'd been into Arizona's looks and style, even if her hostile personality had been about as inviting as skinny-dipping in an icy lake. Like Phoenix, they all admired her.

"Please," he said. "But seriously—you don't want to mess with her, OK?"

"No, I only have to save her zombie soul." I reminded him of the baseline reason we were here. "A lot of people are turning their attention to Arizona since the mystery surrounding Jonas was cleared up. Zoey is, for one."

Phoenix sat up straight. "She's asking questions?"

"Yes, and don't worry, I didn't share any secrets."

He relaxed again.

"Zoey is saying she doesn't believe Arizona drowned herself, and she doesn't think it was an accident either. And I guess she must be right."

"You do?" Mister Cautious gave nothing away, reminding me there were things he couldn't share, even with me.

"Yeah. Otherwise why would Hunter choose her?" I knew the overlord only dealt with injustice and doubt—the random shooting of Summer Madison by an unknown gunman, Phoenix's death by stabbing in a fight between gangs. A straightforward, explicable death didn't deserve all this attention. "She's Beautiful Dead because there's a mystery."

We sat in silence for a while, watching the endless flow of water at our feet.

"Darina, you really don't have to do this." When he spoke, Phoenix had moved away into some remote headspace. "There's a good chance we can find out what happened without you."

I reacted like I'd been stung. "Yeah—like the Beautiful Dead have had ten whole months to do that already, and how far did you get? You only have two months left, remember."

How could we forget? A soul could exist for twelve months in the undead community, not a day more. The end.

"You still don't have to do it."

I stood up and balanced, arms wide, right at the edge of the rock. "What are you saying—that I can have my memory zapped by your superpowers and walk away from here as if you never existed? Good—thanks!"

"The alternative—maybe it's too much to ask." Phoenix offered me an exit from the craziness but I could see in his eyes that he didn't expect me to grab it. He knew better.

"When did I ever walk away?" I murmured.

He kissed me gently this time and stroked the back of my neck. "So you'll help Arizona the way you helped Jonas?"

"Like I will for Summer and for you."

"Then it's time," he said, taking me by the hand.

About the Author

Eden Maguire lives part of the time in the United States where she enjoys the big skies and ice-capped mountains of Colorado. Eden Maguire's lifelong admiration for Emily Brontë's timeless classic, *Wuthering Heights*, ties in with her fascination for the dark side of life and informs her portrayal of the restless, romantic souls in *The Beautiful Dead*. Aside from her interest in the supernatural and the solitary pursuit of writing fiction, Eden's life is lived as much as possible in the outdoors, thanks to ranch-owning friends in Colorado. She says, "Put me on a horse and point me toward a mountain—that's where I find my own personal paradise."